PEARLY AND PIG

AND THE

LOST CITY OF
MU SAVAN

FOR PETER–

my Mekong River travel buddy

First published in 2023
by Walker Books Australia Pty Ltd
Locked Bag 22, Newtown
NSW 2042 Australia
www.walkerbooks.com.au

Walker Books acknowledges the Traditional Owners of the country on which we work, the Gadigal and Wangal peoples of the Eora Nation, and recognises their continuing connection to the land, waters and culture. We pay our respect to their Elders past and present.

A catalogue record for this book is available from the National Library of Australia

ISBN: 978 1 760655 45 7

Typeset in Ovo
Printed and bound in Australia by Griffin Press

10 9 8 7 6 5 4 3 2 1

SUE WHITING

PEARLY AND PIG

AND THE
LOST CITY OF
MU SAVAN

WALKER BOOKS
AND SUBSIDIARIES

LONDON • BOSTON • SYDNEY • AUCKLAND

CHAPTER 1

It was the lush green jungle climbing dizzily from the river that made Pearly Woe's head swirl. She sat at the back of the longboat, gripping the edge of her seat, her shoulders tense, her teeth clenched.

Twisting vines and hungry jungle plants seemed to gobble the ragged hillsides in great leafy gulps. Pearly felt as though she had entered a land that time forgot – an ancient land filled with T-rexes and raptors and brontosauruses. In her mind's eye, she saw enormous pterodactyls circling above. A T-rex thrashing through the jungle tossing wild banana trees out of its way. She could almost hear its roar, feel its hot toothy breath.

Pearly chewed on her bottom lip and willed away the terrifying images. Italian phrases bubbled into her throat – Italian being her go-to language when she was stressed. And, boy, was she stressed.

Mamma mia! she told herself. *Ferma! Stop!*

Pearly couldn't – she wouldn't – let her wild imaginings get in the way. This was her chance to prove herself.

Her parents had called it a "family trip" – a holiday, but Pearly wasn't fooled. This was no family trip or holiday. They were on their way to the village of Ban Noa in the tiny kingdom of Anachak where they would start a long trek through dense jungle in search of the ancient lost city of Mu Savan. A journey through a kingdom with no electricity, no internet, no phone reception, no modern conveniences, to find the ruins of the fabled city her father had been researching for decades. That did not sound like a family "trip" to Pearly. That sounded in every possible way like an adventure. An adventure into the wilds that had already taken two chartered plane trips, one minibus, this longboat and five days to get this far.

And Pearly knew deep within that the only reason she was invited along was so her father could test her. Her father loved setting tests and this was so obviously a test – his way of seeing if her three years of training had paid off. If she had what it took to be an Adventurologist. Pearly clutched her head with both hands and gave it a swift shake. She simply had to stop filling her mind with roaring T-rexes and sharp-clawed raptors ...

Pig wasn't helping. He paced up and down the middle of the boat through the narrow passageway, oinking under his breath, OINKY OINKY NO-NO! OINKY OINKY NO-NO! which was Pig for, *TROUBLE, I SMELL TROUBLE!*

Pearly did not need or want trouble.

She wanted smooth sailing.

She wanted a walk in the park.

She wanted the chance to shine.

Grandpa Woe and her dad, Ricky Woe, sat up the front of the boat beside Pearly's mother, Angel. Angel was perched on a stool behind the boat's wheel, and as usual was giving anyone who would listen a running commentary of the ins and outs of navigating a longboat through the treacherous currents of the Mekong River.

Pearly couldn't hear what her mum was saying above the thrum of the boat's engine, but she could tell by the sheer delight on the faces of her family and the way they were pointing at things and laughing that they were loving every minute of this trip.

Why couldn't she be like that? Why did every bump make her think they had hit a submerged boulder or a hungry crocodile? Why did that luscious jungle only make her wonder where the tigers and snakes and stampeding herds of wild elephants were hiding?

Pig trotted up beside her, his hairs bristling. OINKY OINKY NO-NO! he oinked again.

"What trouble?" Pearly whispered.

I don't know, Pig oinked. *But something isn't right.*

Pearly loved Pig and was proud of his supersonic sniffer and how useful it was, but right now she just wanted reassurance – some positive vibes. Please.

"Maybe you're just excited?" suggested Pearly desperately. "Maybe you're reacting to the fact that we're so close to the village where you were born. So close to seeing your ma."

You think I don't know the difference between excitement and trouble! Pig snorted. *Of course, I'm excited. I can't wait to see Ma. But that's not it. SOMETHING IS WRONG.* Pig squealed that last bit, which only made Pearly's heart thud all the more painfully against her chest. Sometimes having a best friend who had a nose that knows things was tricky!

Just then, Angel cut the engine, and the boat began to drift.

Grandpa Woe stood hands on hips, gazing towards the shore. Her father was frowning. Something *was* wrong. Pig's snout was right again.

Pearly eased herself to her feet and lumbered down the aisle to join them. "What's up?" she asked, her mouth suddenly dry.

"Baffling," said Grandpa Woe. He took off his floppy hat and mopped the sweat off his bald head with the palm of his hand.

"The jetty should be just over there," explained Ricky.

"Near those basalt boulders. But there's no sign of it."

"Maybe it's round the next bend," suggested Angel, turning the wheel vigorously to avoid a sandbar. "The terrain is pretty similar round here. I remember when we visited that time before Pearly was born, there was an extravagant grove of palms along–"

"No," Grandpa Woe cut her short. "I spent almost a year of my life here and I know this is the spot."

"I agree," said Pearly's father. "This certainly feels like the right beach. That limestone peak behind is definitely Elephant Nose–"

OINKY OINKY NO-NO! OINKY OINKY NO-NO! Pig squealed. Pearly crouched beside him and held him close.

"What's Pig saying?" Angel asked Pearly.

"Trouble," said Pearly. "Pig can smell trouble." Pearly was the only one in her family who understood Pig and she felt proud every time she was asked to translate.

"I can't smell it," said Grandpa Woe. "But I can *feel* it. Pig's right. I think we need to investigate. Can you head to shore, Angel?"

Pearly's mother restarted the engine, turned the wheel and edged the boat towards the sandy shoreline. Once in the shallows, Grandpa Woe and Ricky tugged off their boots and socks and launched themselves over the side, as agile as gymnasts. Angel leaned over the rail with a long bamboo pole, using it as a rudder to turn the boat tightly as Ricky and Grandpa Woe guided it onto the shore.

Pearly pulled on her adventure pack. The last time she had pulled on her trusty adventure pack and stepped off a boat like this, she had stepped onto the rocky shores of Antarctica. That had certainly not been a walk in the park. But then she had not been prepared for that adventure – she hadn't trained for it and her adventure pack hadn't even been packed properly. She straightened her shoulders, tightened her straps and clipped on the belt. This time she *was* trained and prepared. This time would be different. She could do this. Couldn't she?

She passed her father and Grandpa Woe their packs, and followed Angel and Pig as they clambered onto dry land.

They all heaved the boat up onto the sand. Angel secured it to a stump poking out of the jungle edge. Ricky wiped his feet with his socks and put his boots back on.

Grandpa Woe didn't bother. He raced across the beach barefooted to the jungle edge, and stood staring at the wall of green, scratching his chin. "Curious," he said, then, "Perplexing."

Ricky joined him, his ageing map of the area in hand. "There should be a track somewhere here. I remember it distinctly. But there's no sign of it."

Pearly and Pig wandered along the beach, Pig with his snout to the sand, oinking, OINKY OINKY NO-NO! OINKY OINKY NO-NO! He sniffed and oinked and sniffed and oinked until he stopped suddenly beside a broken-down bamboo structure concealed beneath a clutch of ferns and vines.

Pearly and Pig's eyes zeroed in on the strange structure, then on each other.

"Grandpa Woe!" Pearly called urgently.

Grandpa Woe, Ricky and Angel jogged up the beach and peered at the strange structure. Grandpa's weather-beaten face was furrowed with worry. He rubbed again at his stubbly chin.

"Curiouser and curiouser," he said.

"The remains of the jetty," elaborated Ricky, checking between his crumpled map, his compass and the scene before him. "Which means the track to Ban Noa is directly in front of us."

They all turned to where Grandpa Woe was already pointing.

But there was no track. Just dense impenetrable jungle.

"*Mamma mia*," breathed Pearly.

OINKY OINKY NO-NO! oinked Pig.

He was darn right.

CHAPTER 2

Pearly cast suspicious eyes over the tangly jungle that bordered the beach. *Anything could be hiding in there,* she fretted. *A nest of writhing venomous snakes. Or spotted leopards ready to pounce. Or strangler vines poised to strangle. Or killer ticks waiting to kill.*

Pearly took a step backwards. It was obvious they couldn't get through. So what were they waiting for? She turned, ready to flee.

"Machete," said Angel.

The word stopped Pearly mid-flee.

"It's not rocket science." Angel drew her machete from her pack and strode towards the thick foliage. "We just need to cut a new path."

"Mamma mia!" muttered Pearly.

"Steady on," said Grandpa Woe. "We must tread lightly."

"Father's right," said Ricky. "Let's think this through and come up with a plan that will minimise impact so the vegetation will restore swiftly."

Restore swiftly? Pearly took another backwards step. *Slam shut on them as they pass through, more likely.*

Angel's eyes twinkled with amusement. "Oh, come on, you guys. We've done this before." She laughed and winked at Pearly's father. "Surely, we don't need to do a ten-page essay on the advantages and disadvantages of cutting a narrow path through the jungle." She elbowed Ricky playfully and swiped at the leafy branch in front of her. "We know the drill. Cut only what's necessary. Minimum impact. Tread lightly." *Slash. Slash.* A thin path was already emerging. "There's obviously something not right here. Something rotten in the Kingdom of Anachak. Even Pig knows it."

Pig snorted at the "even Pig" reference.

"Don't worry, Pig," said Grandpa Woe. "We don't take your nose for *grunt*ed!" Grandpa Woe chuckled. Pig kicked out his hind legs and Pearly rolled her eyes. "But, seriously," Grandpa Woe continued, "Angel does have a point."

"Well, I guess this is a good opportunity for Pearly to practise her machete skills," said her father.

Pearly gulped. "Shouldn't someone mind the boat?"

Grandpa Woe shook his head, laughing, as he tipped sand out of his boots and tugged them on.

"Come up front, Pearly," said Angel. "Your father's right. This is a perfect opportunity."

9

Pig rubbed his side against Pearly's legs. *You've got this*, he encouraged. *Remember – smoky bacon! Smoky bacon to your worries.*

Pearly drew in a deep breath. S*moky bacon* was Pig's way of venting when he was frustrated or upset and it had become a special phrase for Pearly too. Repeating the piggy cursing had helped to settle her nerves many times before and it had certainly got her through their Antarctic adventure only a couple of months ago.

Smoky bacon to my worries, Pearly said to herself, grinning her thanks to Pig. *Smoky bacon, smoky bacon*, she repeated, as she took hold of the handle of her machete.

"We can slice in tandem," said her mother. "Just like we did in the bamboo forest on Orchard Island during our prep. Got it? You go first."

Pearly appreciated her mother's guidance. She sometimes wondered why Angel – and her dad and grandpa – hadn't given up on her long ago. She had somehow fluked it through her adventure in Antarctica and had unwittingly saved the day, but other than that she had shown no talent at anything as an Adventurologist-in-training – other than languages. (She was proficient in twenty-seven languages, including some animal languages.) But what use were languages when faced with a hungry boa constrictor or a sheer ravine or an impenetrable fog – or a solid wall of tangled vines and thick jungle plants, like now.

Oh, smoky bacon, this was no way to prove herself. She was faltering already – she just hadn't imagined that her first step would be slashing her way through the jungle. She had imagined a different landscape: wide well-worn paths, fringed with waving coconut palms shading her from the sun.

Instead, insects screamed. Birds screeched from the tops of trees. And sweat trickled down Pearly's back as she swung the machete at the base of the plant in front of her. It took a couple of goes but eventually it fell to the ground.

"Tread lightly," reminded Grandpa Woe. "Keep the path needle thin."

"Take care with that blade," warned her father, mopping sweat from his brow.

Pig lagged behind, keeping well clear of the swinging machetes and falling branches, but Pearly could hear him muttering as he sniffed frantically on both sides of the track.

OINKY-OINKY. GRUNT-SQUEAKITY-SQUEAK-SQUEALIO. HOR HOR INK, oinked Pig, which was Pig for, *Still trouble. And a new scent. Not human ... monkey, I think.*

That was not totally unexpected, they were in the jungle after all. It was full of all types of monkeys.

The terrain rose sharply from the river, the ground underfoot mossy and slippery. This was hot, hard work. Pearly slapped at the bitey insects swarming around her. She wiped her brow with her sleeve. Her hair was wet under her hat and limp curls stuck to her cheeks. Her mother was swinging with gusto, telling Pearly all about the last time they had visited Ban Noa.

"It was well before you were born, Pearly. Actually, it was my last adventure before I fell pregnant with you. King Alung Chu was so welcoming and your father became chums with young Prince Keej ..." Pearly tuned out. She'd heard the story many times before.

Pearly's hands were getting sweat-slippery. She stopped for a moment to wipe them on her trousers. Grandpa Woe and her father were trudging quite a few steps behind, keeping well away from the swinging blades. Grandpa Woe tossed a cut branch into the undergrowth and stepped carefully over a clutch of tiny ferns. Her father was too engrossed in his map and antique compass and was not paying such attention. So much so, he tripped on a tree root, and tumbled over.

"Dang," he cursed.

Grandpa Woe held out his hand to help him up. "Put the map away, lad," he said. "And watch where you're going. We need to respect the jungle." Pearly giggled. She loved it when Grandpa Woe treated her father like a little kid.

Ricky grumbled as he folded the crumpled map and dusted off his trousers.

Just then, her mother gave out a little shriek, at the same moment as Pig squealed, *Monkeys. Lots of them.*

Pearly's eyes flew from her mother to Pig and back again as she stumbled out of the jungle onto flatter moss-covered ground and into a clearing of sorts. They had broken through!

Ricky and Grandpa Woe bounded up to join them.

"No," breathed Grandpa Woe.

"Where have they gone?" said Angel, hands on hips.

Pearly gawked open-mouthed at the scene before her. The remnants of bamboo huts on wonky stilts dotted the clearing, though they were hard to spot with the snaky vines and wide-leafed jungle plants winding their way through the open windows and broken doors. And monkeys – macaque monkeys – were everywhere. Silent and staring. Perched on roof tops, on window ledges, under buildings, on branches, long tails swinging.

"This is – *was* – the village of Ban Noa, Pearly," Ricky whispered, out of the side of his mouth, his eyes darting from side to side. "This is the village where your grandpa lived all those years ago. Where your mother and I have stayed a number of times too."

"Deserted. Absolutely deserted and consumed by the jungle. And overrun by those monkeys." Angel slid her machete into its sheath. "I have an uneasy feeling about this."

Pig snorted his agreement.

Grandpa Woe had nothing to say. He took off his hat and held it against his stomach. Tears welled in his eyes, as he wandered off into what remained of the village. He peered into windows. Touched walls. Crouched and looked underneath the buildings. Pearly's eyes moistened too. Grandpa Woe rarely got emotional like this.

Suddenly, one large macaque scrambled to the top of a bare branch that hung over the centre of the village. He raised his head into the air, shook the branch fiercely, bared his teeth, large fangs glistening, and screeched.

It was so loud it sent a shiver down Pearly's spine.

He shook the branch again – even more fiercely – and let fly with another deafening screech.

It was a warning.

A threat.

A call to action.

CHAPTER 3

Instantly, the troop responded. Monkeys leapt from roof to roof, branch to branch - flying through the air - hissing and screaming and barking.

Pearly tried to make out what they were saying. They were mighty agitated, that's for sure. *Danger! Beware! Hide the children!* And most worrying of all - the constant cries of: *Fight!*

The squawks whirled noisily around Pearly. She bent down and held Pig close.

But Grandpa Woe seemed not to notice. He stood in the middle of the abandoned Ban Noa and gazed, open-mouthed, all around him, oblivious to the monkeys, who were becoming increasingly aggressive and bold.

Just then, two large monkeys swooped out of a tree, landing right behind Pig who squealed and shot out of Pearly's arms. Pearly fell backwards onto the ground, as Pig fled to join Grandpa Woe. A gang of six or seven screeching monkeys approached Pearly and her parents. Pearly scrambled to her feet, her pulse racing. The gang kept advancing, their threats becoming louder, their fangs rising out of their open mouths like deadly spears. Angel and Ricky and Pearly backed away, inching towards Grandpa Woe and Pig.

"Can you understand them?" Angel whispered to Pearly, taking hold of her shaking hand.

"A bit. They feel threatened. We're trespassing on their patch, I think. The first one shouted something like, *battle* or *fight*. And now the others are saying the same."

"That's what I was afraid of," whispered Angel as the three joined Grandpa Woe and Pig.

It was then that Pearly realised that the monkeys had herded them to this spot. A seething mass of screeching, screaming monkeys, tails raised, teeth flashing, stood on all sides. They were surrounded.

"Can you communicate with them?" Angel asked.

Pearly had met many macaques on her trips to Singapore to visit her grandmother, Esmeralda. She tried to recall her conversations with them in the nature reserve that bordered Esmeralda's estate, but the noise of the troop was making it difficult to think straight, and her tongue felt too thick in her mouth to speak.

The monkeys edged closer, closing in on all sides.

"Pearly?" pleaded her mother. "Please. Say something – anything. Tell them we come in peace."

"You can do it," said Grandpa Woe. The first words

he had spoken since they stepped foot in the deserted Ban Noa.

Pearly let go of her mother's hand and took a tentative step forwards.

Smoky bacon to your worries, Pig squeaked kindly.

Pearly swallowed. She tried to push away the Italian phrases that were churning through her and instead concentrate on finding the right sounds and gestures to make.

Cautiously, she knelt on one shaky knee, bowed her head and put her trembling hands to her chest to show she was not challenging the troop.

The dominant monkey, still perched on the dead branch, screeched. *Fight! Fight! Fight!*

Pearly felt as if she might dissolve into a puddle, but she remained kneeling, not daring to look above her.

"I think we should all kneel. Don't make eye contact," she said out of the corner of her mouth, hoping her family could hear over the racket the monkeys were making.

Pearly sensed movement beside her. She snuck a glance and almost giggled when she spied Pig trying to kneel. She swallowed the giggle down; she didn't want to break the spell, because the troop was settling, the noise diminishing.

The dominant male hurled ear-splitting screeches at them.

Pearly wasn't certain what they all meant, but they seemed to be telling her that this was their turf and the humans should get the heck out of here.

Pearly agreed. She moistened her lips, and without raising her head, attempted to find the right noises to reply something along the lines of: *We will go. We are sorry.*

GO NOW! screeched the male.

GO! GO! GO! screeched the mob of monkeys surrounding them, who had once again started flicking their tails and hissing and leaping about with agitation.

"Go!" yelled Pearly. "We have to go." She stumbled up and grabbed hold of her mother's hand. "Quickly!"

Grandpa Woe stayed kneeling. "Ask them first. Ask them what happened to the village."

"Grandpa ..." He couldn't mean it, surely.

"Please," he said, his voice croaky.

Pearly drew in a deep breath. She kept her eyes downcast, but moved her arms so they hung gently at her sides. She turned towards the dominant male, without catching his eye, looking humble and submissive, and made a series of soft monkey chattering sounds that she hoped would convey *The humans? The village? What happened?*

The dominant male sat back on his haunches and scraped his upper canines over thin black lips. He huffed then squawked, *Gone!* And pointed up to the mountain. *Gone!*

Pearly relayed his answer to the others, as the dominant male flopped back onto all fours, shook the branch and screeched: *Go! Go!*

"We have to go!" cried Pearly. "Hurry!"

They all scrambled to their feet. Pearly raced towards the jungle path they had just made. The ring of monkeys broke apart to let her through, but they continued to gallop around her, herding her, harassing her. Pig trotted close by. Ricky bounded past and then Angel, white-faced and wide-eyed, her red curls streaming behind her.

But where was Grandpa Woe?

Pearly glanced over her shoulder as she ran.

The screeching and squawking escalated, as the troop suddenly turned and charged off in the opposite direction.

The four stopped at the jungle edge, bewildered.

Then Pearly spotted what had got them worked up again.

Grandpa Woe was heading across to the opposite side of the village, his machete drawn. He was going to slash his way up into those mountains.

CHAPTER 4

"Father!" yelled Ricky. "What are you doing?"

"He's going to find the people of Ban Noa, of course," said Angel, her eyes lighting up, her voice fizzing with excitement. "Which is what we *all* should be doing. They might be in trouble. They might need our help. Remember the charter: *No adventure too small. No challenge too great!*" She pulled out her machete. "Come on!" She twirled round and grinned at them. "What are you waiting for?"

Pearly, her father and Pig all watched her go.

Pearly knew they should follow her mother and help Grandpa Woe. That's what you did on adventures, didn't you? But a bigger part of her wanted to charge down that track and not stop until she was back on board their boat.

She latched eyes with her father. Ricky was chewing his lips furiously and appeared equally torn. He rubbed his hand over the deep frowning creases between his eyes and then fiddled with his neck scarf, shaking his head and muttering what sounded like, *I knew this was a mistake.*

"Perhaps we should get you and Pig back to the boat?" he said finally. This was not what Pearly had expected.

"And leave Mum and Grandpa Woe?" Now that her father had put voice to the idea, it sounded so terribly wrong. Woes didn't desert the ship. They helped each other, didn't they? "We can't do that ... can we?"

Ma, Pig oinked desperately.

"And what about Pig's ma?" added Pearly. "Pig's worried."

Ricky's shoulders slumped with defeat. "I suppose we don't have much choice," he said and clicked his tongue. He pulled out his machete, held it high and then grabbed onto Pearly with his free hand. "Keep your head down and stay close. You too, Pig! Come on."

Pearly's father charged across the village, waving his machete above his head, hauling Pearly along. Pearly floundered behind him, like a caught fish being dragged in on a line, her eyes sliding across the broken-down, jungle-strangled village, past the mass of squabbling, screeching monkeys all around them, to the jungle edge and beyond – up to the jagged limestone mountain peaks that pierced thick pads of white cloud. Were they really going up there?

Pig bumped into Pearly, stumbled, then tumbled and stumbled some more. He was making a low AROO, AROO, AROO. It made Pearly's skin tingle. It was the sound he made when he was stressed – which only made Pearly all the more stressed too. This adventure was going from bad to worse.

Expect the unexpected, the words from the *RAG – The Rules and Guidelines for Young Adventurologists* – thudded against her skull. *Do adventures have to be this unexpected?* Pearly grumbled.

"Keep up, Pig! Keep close, Pearly!" Ricky called above the noise of the monkeys, which was changing from high-pitched squeals to low grunts and bird-like chittering. He swung his machete and whooped some more. By the time the three had made their way to the jungle that fringed what used to be Ban Noa, the macaques seemed to be losing interest in them. Only a few remained, jumping about, hissing and barking at Grandpa Woe: *Go! Go! Go!* The others had either melted into the jungle or were perched on rooftops and branches watching the scene unfold below them, chittering like a band of gossips.

Grandpa Woe and Angel had made good progress. Already, they were barely visible from the village. The only sign of their presence was the top of Grandpa Woe's faded orange hat and the flash of Angel's red curls, popping up occasionally above the fern fronds and vines. That, and the strong and rhythmic chop of their machetes. Grandpa Woe was almost seventy, but he was as strong as most thirty-year-olds. And Angel was stronger than them all. Pearly pulled herself free from her father's grip and scooted along the thread of a track to catch up to them.

"Grandpa Woe," Pearly called. "Where are you going?"

Grandpa Woe stopped swinging. He wiped his brow with the edge of his cotton shirt and turned to face his family, who were all standing shoulder to shoulder now, squashed into the tight path Grandpa Woe and Angel had cut.

"The people of Ban Noa are like a second family to me," he said, his voice gravelly. "They nursed me back to health after my caving accident. I've spent months of my life with them. King Alung Chu is like a brother. I can't just walk away. I have to find them."

Grandpa Woe craned his neck to see if any macaques were following, then leant up against a tree trunk, breathing deeply to catch his breath.

"But Father, do you have a plan? Do you have one scrap of evidence that you are going in the right direction?" Ricky dropped his pack to the ground and pulled out his ancient map, manoeuvring himself in a tight circle until he had enough room to open it up. Pearly shook her head. Her father loved his maps.

Loved his plans. He thought every problem could be solved with a map and a plan.

"Calm down, lad," said Grandpa Woe. "Planning is important. Being prepared is one of the basics of Adventurologing, as we all know – and so too is being spontaneous when things don't go to plan."

Grandpa Woe was quoting the *RAG*. Pearly felt he was doing it for her benefit, not for her father's.

"Besides," added Angel. "This is a sticky situation – and we all know that in sticky situations you need to *act quickly* and *take initiative* in order to survive them."

Again, words from the *RAG*. Words Pearly knew by heart and words that she had to convince her family that she knew – and understood – or she would never be an Adventurologist in her family's eyes. She felt like such a learner, she may as well have yellow and black "L" plates strapped to her back.

"Let's not forget Number 7 of 'Surviving Sticky Situations' then: *don't panic*," said Ricky. "And Father, honestly, you are absolutely panicking here. You are levering everything on a grunt and bark of a cranky primate and that cranky primate pointing vaguely in this direction. We should go back to the boat and think this through. To work out a plan. To be prepared. This is so unlike you."

Grandpa stood and slashed at the base of a vine

swaying in front of him. "Do what you wish, lad. But do it without me."

"And me," said Angel. She adjusted her adventure pack on her back and joined Grandpa Woe.

Ricky shook his head. "This is not cool. This is outside the Guild's Charter – that *you* wrote!" He folded his map carefully, put it in the front pocket of his pack and slung the pack over one shoulder. "And for the record, I think this is *utter* foolishness." He stomped off, following his wife and father, flinging branches out of the way angrily. "And it is putting us all in unnecessary danger."

OINK-GOO-OINK, oinked Pig, which was Pig for *Smoky bacon!* Pig snorted then added, *He's in a huff.*

"Tell me about it," replied Pearly.

"Come on, Pearly," called Angel, "more slashing practice awaits."

Mamma mia! Pearly swiped wet strands of hair from her forehead and pushed through the overhanging banana leaves to join Angel, reminding herself that this was no family holiday. This was a test. And if she was ever going to lose those "L" plates, she was going to have to do her bit.

Hopefully, with the monkeys behind us, she thought, *things will go more smoothly*.

Of course, she was wrong.

CHAPTER 5

The sun was high in the sky. Pearly's head throbbed. Her stomach grumbled. She had been slashing for at least an hour. She slid her pack off her aching shoulders, and it hit the ground with a whump. She sheathed her machete and pressed her back up against a tree, just off the track. Her mother kept slashing, her swings, and also her chatter not missing a beat, unaware Pearly had stopped. Her grandfather was bent over examining delicate fern fronds poking out of the leaf matter and her father was frowning with concentration at his map and compass.

"Father," he said, without looking up, "do you think the deserted Ban Noa has suffered the same fate as Mu Savan? Is it possible that history is repeating itself?"

Grandpa Woe clapped her father on the shoulder. "I doubt it, lad. But anything is possible." They passed right by her without noticing.

Pearly was too tired and hungry to care. She unzipped the front pocket of her pack and pulled out a banana. Pig plopped beside her, panting, drool bubbling out of his mouth and dripping in long strings to puddle on the ground.

Monkey, he oinked softly, once the others were well out of view, her mother's voice barely more than a soft rolling drone.

"Yes, there're lots of monkeys," said Pearly, her eyebrows knitted with annoyance. She was too hot and bothered for useless conversations.

No, one *monkey. Following us. Has been for quite some time. Don't look up, but it's right above you.*

Pearly looked up, and her eyes caught a pair of round golden-brown eyes within an impish face, framed by two pointy ears. The monkey opened its mouth wide and yawned, then climbed along a narrow branch, its tail swinging.

"Are you sure it's following us?" Pearly whispered.

Pig clicked his tongue. *Absolutely*, he oinked.

Without thinking, Pearly pushed her way through long wet leaves and under a string of thorny vines to stand below where the monkey now sat.

She put her hands to her chest and made some friendly chittering and squeaking noises that she hoped said, *Hello. Are you looking for food?*

The monkey tilted its head from one side to the other. It grabbed a handful of leaves and shoved them in its mouth. It stared down at Pearly.

27

Pearly tried again.

Nice leaves, she squeaked. *But look.* She held up the banana.

Cheekiness lit the monkey's face. It was definitely a youngster. Not yet fully grown.

Pearly held the banana higher. Like lightning, the little macaque flew from the branch, grabbed the banana out of her grasp and leapt back up into the tree. It chittered and squeaked – *arr-arr-ooo-ooo, arr-arr-ooo-ooo* – sounding like a kookaburra, reminding her of the mainland back home. And like a kookaburra, Pearly knew it was laughing at her.

The monkey peeled the banana, swallowed the creamy insides in one gulp, then tossed the skin at Pearly, the skin landing – *splat* – on Pearly's upturned face.

Pearly yelped. Pig shot from the track and trotted through the undergrowth to join her.

Are you okay? he oinked.

"Yep. Just a wayward banana skin." Pearly peeled the skin from her face and tried to gather herself. "And a mischievous monkey." She was glad Pig was close by.

Arr-arr-goo-goo, the monkey laughed. *Banana head! Banana head!*

Pearly ignored the jibe. *Are you lost?* she chittered to the monkey. *Have you lost your family?*

That got a reaction. The monkey raised itself up on two legs and sprang to another tree, then it swung from limb to limb and back again, chattering and squawking: *Lost! No. I look after troop! I make sure you go, go, go!* It broke off a branch and tossed it at Pearly. It seemed she had offended him.

OINKY OINKY NO-NO! Pig squealed. *This monkey is trouble*, he added.

"Yep," Pearly whispered to Pig. "But this monkey knows something, I reckon."

Sorry, Pearly chattered to the monkey, trying to keep the tone friendly.

You are lost, banana head, the monkey squawked back, in a far from friendly tone.

Not lost, Pearly replied. *Looking for the humans.*

Bah! The monkey hissed. *Lost! Lost! Lost! Bah!*

Pearly's eyes swept from side to side, taking in what the monkey said. *Do you know where they are?* she asked.

Yes! I am Wah-Wah! I know everything. You are banana head. You know nothing. I will be the troop boss one day.

Wah-Wah was bossy and rude and full of himself, that's for sure. But he might also be helpful.

"Pearly! *Pearly!* Where are you?" It was her father. He sounded panicked as well as huffy now. But his timing couldn't be worse, because there was a rustle of leaves and a swish of a branch and Wah-Wah was gone.

Dang, thought Pearly.

She glimpsed her father on the track they had cut, hands on hips, looking around.

You're in trouble, Pig oinked, scurrying off to join Ricky.

"Thanks, friend," mumbled Pearly as she unsnagged sharp thorns from her shirt sleeve and stepped over the small understorey plants, suddenly aware of the possibility of vipers or spiders hiding underneath, and made her way back to the track. What had she been thinking?

Ricky's face was flushed from the heat. He mopped it with his neck scarf. "What on earth were you doing off track?"

"There's a monkey from Ban Noa. He's been following us. I wanted to know why."

"Great – let's all stop and chat to the primates. I don't know what's got into this family."

Pearly didn't know what had got into her father, who was usually so calm and cool and level-headed.

Ricky sighed. "You must stay with the group, Pearly. Like Pig, I have a bad feeling about this. And this is not just any ordinary adventure. It is an important one to me. Mu Savan has been an obsession of mine since I was not much older than you and came here with Father – and I finally have a good idea where the ruin of the city might be hidden. Please don't veer off like that again. I have enough to contend with – with the people from Ban Noa missing, and all. A complication no one foresaw."

Pearly was stunned into silence – her father was almost rambling. Was it the heat? But before she could reply, there was a sudden whoosh as Wah-Wah swung across the track right over the top of their heads. Ricky grabbed Pearly and dived them both to the ground, as if escaping a bomb blast. Wah-Wah landed in the branches of a young palm and started his kookaburra impersonation again, *arr-arr-ooo-ooo, arr-arr-ooo-oooo!* Pig joined him, rolling onto his back and doing his piggy snort-laugh.

Pearly pulled out of her father's hold and stood up, brushing leaves and sticks from her pants, and shaking her head.

"That's Wah-Wah, the macaque from Ban Noa," Pearly explained to a slightly embarrassed Ricky, who was adjusting his hat, straightening his neck scarf and not making eye contact.

Pearly gave Wah-Wah a playful grunt and squeal, telling him he was cheeky.

"Come on," said Ricky. "We best catch up with the others."

Pig rolled onto his feet and trotted up the track. Pearly went to follow him but Wah-Wah barked, fiercely shaking the palm branch he was perched on.

Pearly stopped and cocked her head to one side. *What?* she chittered.

The little macaque jumped up and down on the spot. *Wrong way, banana head! Wrong way!* he squeaked and chittered. *Humans that way.* He pointed to the north-west of where Grandpa Woe was heading.

Can you show us? Pearly asked, shoulders hunched and hands upturned in question.

Follow Wah-Wah. Bring bananas!

Bring bananas! Wah-Wah brought new meaning to the phrase "cheeky monkey", that was for sure.

CHAPTER 6

It was no easy task to persuade her family to follow Wah-Wah. But in the end, they agreed. After all, they were only following the vague direction that the troop's leader had pointed them in anyhow, and after almost an hour of slashing and trekking, they hadn't found any evidence of human activity, Pig's sniffer confirming this. So perhaps they *were* going in the wrong direction. *What did they have to lose?* they decided eventually. *Following Wah-Wah couldn't hurt, could it? Unless he had other motives, and that was unlikely from a bold, juvenile monkey, surely?*

Wah-Wah chittered and chattered as he danced through the trees and across the jungle canopy. He moved gracefully, stopping now and then to point and to BAH-OOO-BAH-OOO, BAH-OOO-BAH-OOO, which more or less told Pearly which way to go and at the same time to complain about how slow her humans were. Why couldn't they just swing from tree to tree like him?

Pearly cast her eyes up through the trees. The jungle was even denser here. Tree trunks, wound with creepers and vines, thrust from ground to sky, their canopy so thick it was as if the jungle was wearing an enormous floppy sunhat, casting the family in deep shade. Slim shafts of light stabbed through occasional gaps here and there spotlighting the ground below. And the air was as thick as the jungle itself, so humid it was hard to breathe. Sweat dripped from Pearly's face and ran down her back and chest, her shirt wet and clinging.

Angel and Ricky plodded up ahead. They both looked done in. Grandpa Woe was the only one slashing and chopping now, and he did so with unwavering energy.

"I remember this section of the jungle. Not far from that peak over there is the cave system I got trapped in back in '84." Grandpa Woe was unusually chatty, taking over from Angel's commentary. And this from the man who believed using ten words when one would do was a waste. "I think your little Wah-Wah knows where he's going," he continued. "I am almost certain the jungle thins out up ahead, into a shallow bowl of a valley. I remember it distinctly because it was so unusual for the area, in geological terms, that is. A bowl edged by thin limestone pillars, like enormous stalagmites you'd find in a cave – completely engulfed by the jungle of course, but visible to those who cared to look carefully enough. Ancient, eroded mountain peaks, I presume."

Pearly trudged on. She had been tasked with communicating with Wah-Wah, and keeping him supplied with bananas from their packs. Pig was tasked with sniffing out humans – and trouble. But hopefully not both! Pearly felt slightly encouraged – perhaps this adventure was back on track. This could be her chance to shine and prove herself to her parents, after all. Maybe ...

Above her, Wah-Wah hung from a vine with one arm. He chittered and squeaked and pointed, indicating that they should head towards a large round boulder that was just coming in sight. Pearly shouted instructions to Grandpa Woe, who diverted his slashing slightly to the right to take the most direct route.

Pig was panting again and lagging behind. He didn't like the heat. Which was rather weird seeing as he was born here. Though Pearly wondered if he was lagging because of worry for his mother, rather than heat stress.

Pearly took off her hat and shook the sweat from her curls as she looked about for Wah-Wah. The little monkey was nowhere to be seen. Pearly turned in a circle, peering through the branches, her heart pumping fast.

Uh-oh, had she spoken too soon? Something was wrong.

Pig confirmed it. He raced up to where Pearly was standing.

OINKY OINKY NO-NO! It was more of a screech than an oink and it was full of panic. *Trouble! I smell trouble. And humans! And–*

He didn't get to finish because, right at that moment, Angel screamed.

Pearly and Pig raced up the track, leaping over rotting logs and newly cut branches, only to come to an abrupt stop as soon as they rounded the bend.

Grandpa Woe, Angel and Ricky had their hands raised in the air. Blocking their way was a band of six people, all waving spears and shouting in Anachakan.

Their words were so fast and angry, Pearly was having trouble understanding them. She had learnt the language from Grandpa Woe but had never heard it spoken by native speakers before. Regardless, she understood enough to know that they considered the family trespassers – and now they were all prisoners. Had Wah-Wah led them into a trap? Had she been wrong to trust him?

Pearly scanned the canopy to look for the monkey – but he was still nowhere to be seen. *The little blighter.*

Grandpa Woe, with hands still raised, stepped towards the angry group. They shouted at him to stop, but he kept going, talking to them softly and calmly in Anachakan. "Hello! I am Gordon Woe. A friend of

King Alung Chu. A friend of the people of Ban Noa ..."
Surprise at Grandpa speaking their language showed
immediately on their faces – they looked at one another,
eyebrows drawn, frowning. Grandpa continued. "We
found the village deserted. We were worried for you. I
am so pleased to have found you. Relieved! Please take
me to see King Alung Chu – he will explain."

This mention of the king seemed to anger the
group. They shouted at Grandpa that he was no friend
of Ban Noa and that he was a liar.

"Do not speak of the former king. It is forbidden,"
said the man at the front of the pack, who seemed to
be the leader.

"Former king?" Grandpa Woe's voice wobbled.
"What happened to him?"

"He is gone and that is that. We do not look back.
We look forward. This is ordered by King Foom Chu."

"Foom Chu is the king?"

The leader didn't respond. Instead, he nodded
at a lean, muscly woman who was standing atop the
boulder at the side of the track. She scampered down
the boulder and gestured for them to hand over
their machetes. Pearly stood stock still. The woman
wrenched Pearly's machete out of its sleeve, in one
purposeful action that left Pearly trembling.

When the woman spotted Pig, she stopped dead.
Then she smiled, put her palms together and bowed.

She called out, "*Chu-la! Chu-la! Chu-la!*" which was Anachakan for *Pig! Pig! Pig!* The gang turned and bowed at Pig.

Pig made surprised squealing noises, his tail wagging. Pearly was bewildered.

"Pigs are sacred in the Kingdom of Anachak. They are their totem," Grandpa Woe explained. "He might just be our saviour," he whispered grimly.

The leader gave another nod and the rest of the group huddled around the family and prodded them with their spears, instructing them to walk.

Where are they taking us? Pearly worried. In her mind's eye she saw them all tied to a palm tree and left to bake in the sun. She shook free of that image only for it to be replaced by a scene of them being thrown into a pit of deadly black scorpions.

Pig kept close to Pearly's side. As they made their way past the boulder and onto a well-worn track, Pig nudged her legs frantically with his snout.

Pearly, he oinked softly. *I can smell pigs – lots and lots of pigs.* There was so much hopefulness in his voice that tears welled in Pearly's eyes. Maybe all was not lost. Maybe Pig will be reunited with his ma. And maybe, like Grandpa Woe just said, maybe Pig will be key to getting them out of this mess.

Pearly adjusted her pack on her back and crossed her fingers and toes. They needed something to go their way.

CHAPTER 7

Grandpa Woe was spot on with his recollections – and his prediction. Once they passed the boulder, the jungle opened up. First into a wide track, the canopy thinning and allowing the baking sun to stream down on them. The track led them into the bowl-shaped clearing Grandpa Woe had spoken about, and the new location of the village of Ban Noa.

The village sat huddled in the floor of the clearing, surrounded on three sides by vine-covered pointy fingers of rock, green with moss and lichen. It was as if the village was being held by a large green hand, and to Pearly it felt suffocating, as if the fingers of rock were ready to fold together and squeeze tight, trapping them within. She swallowed hard.

The prisoners and their captors trudged single file across a swaying bamboo bridge over a trickly creek. As they stepped off the bridge, ear-splitting grunting and oinking exploded from deep within the village.

Pig lifted his snout in the air. His ears alert. His curly tail wagging with anticipation. The village was alive with pigs. Pink pigs, spotted pigs, black and white splotched pigs – an abundance of pigs, of every shape and size – galloped and trotted and cavorted towards them, grunting and snorting and kicking up massive clouds of orange dust.

The leader held up his spear and stopped the group. When the pigs approached, he bowed deeply to them. Then he whistled shrilly, held up one palm and said in Anachakan to the pigs, "Stop. Make way."

The pigs sniffed and snorted and wiggled their behinds until they had made a path through the middle of them. *A welcoming party perhaps?* Pearly wondered.

The leader bowed to the pigs again, then turned, and raised his spear into the air. "Walk!" he commanded his prisoners. His prisoners obeyed.

The noise of the pigs was deafening – even worse than the macaques in the old Ban Noa – and Pearly's nerves were making it difficult for her to put one foot in front of the other.

Her eyes fell on Pig, who was trotting ahead. His snout was held so high that it must have been hard for him to see where he was going, and his tail still wagged furiously, as if he was king of the pigs! Maybe he was. His mother *was* the Divine Sow. And soon he would be reunited with her.

40

Angel and Ricky glanced behind, raised their eyebrows at Pig and grinned.

Her father caught Pearly's eye. *You okay?* he mouthed.

Hold tight, whispered her mother.

Pearly tried to smile back reassuringly.

The leader marched them through the village, which bore little resemblance to the deserted Ban Noa that had been overrun with jungle plants and cranky monkeys. The jungle here was held back from the village by the strange rocky pillars and there was not a single monkey in sight. Not even Wah-Wah, which annoyed Pearly. Had that little monkey fooled her? But why would he do that? He couldn't have known they would be taken prisoner, surely, she reasoned. But the thought that she had been the one who led her family into this mess did not rest easily on her conscience.

Several neat rows of tidy bamboo huts stood on stilts across the clearing, with wide dirt pathways between them. The pathways led directly towards an imposing fence.

This Ban Noa seemed much more organised than the old Ban Noa. But there was something very strange and deeply disturbing about it. It wasn't the abundance of pigs or the strange fingers of rock that enclosed the village. It was the lack of human activity. A few hens strutted about and pecked at the ground, and pigs could be seen everywhere, but other than the gang who had captured them and were marching them towards the fence, Pearly couldn't spot a single human – not a single man, woman or child. Though she felt eyes upon her and at times thought she glimpsed someone peeking out of a window or doorway.

"Pig, can you smell human?" Pearly whispered.

Yes, many. They appear to be hiding. But they are all around.

That made the hairs on the back of her neck stand up. She recalled the stories Grandpa Woe had told her about Ban Noa. How friendly everyone was. He made it sound like paradise, an idyllic life on the river, catching fish, foraging for fruit and everyone in the village working, eating and playing together. Singing and dancing at night, telling stories, helping each other. She wondered what Grandpa Woe was thinking. She willed him to look behind, so she could see the expression on his face, but he marched purposefully behind the leader, his step never faltering, his gaze straight ahead.

"What about Wah-Wah?" she asked Pig, but was prodded with the end of a spear and told to be quiet.

Regardless, Pig oinked back. *No Wah-Wah. Just humans and hens and glorious pigs – many cousins – but also lots of trouble!*

Pearly was not surprised. She didn't have a supersonic sniffer like Pig, but she could sense trouble in this place too. As her mother had said earlier, there was something rotten happening in the Kingdom of Anachak.

They had reached the fence and Pearly's anxieties grew wings.

The fence was made of sharpened bamboo poles and stretched across the entire width of the village, wedging at both ends against mossy pillars of rock that soared out of the ground like the massive stalagmites Grandpa Woe spoke about. An unexpected tangle of razor wire ran across the top of the spear-like poles and torches flamed all along, black strings of smoke curling into the air and tickling Pearly's nose.

Their captors stopped the Woes in front of an impressive wooden gate with a carving of an enormous and very regal-looking pig carved across it. Pearly studied it closely.

The Divine Sow! Pig oinked happily, his tail wagging picking up pace. *Ma*, he whispered wistfully.

The gate creaked open to a large compound, where at least ten hefty guards stood, all holding spears.

"In!" one of them commanded in Anachakan.

Pearly gulped. There was no way in the world that Pearly wanted to step inside that compound. Anything could happen in there. And once inside, Pearly worried there would be no way out. No escape. Waves of panic mushroomed inside her – just like they had that time she was stuck in the ice cave in Antarctica. She took deep calming breaths and tried to will away the panic, and make her feet work, but she was stuck fast.

The sharp end of a spear prodded just under her ribs. She turned her frightened eyes towards the spear holder.

"Inside," he said, his voice gruff, and prodded her again.

She obeyed. She took several wonky steps into the compound and joined Pig and her family, who were lined up in front of the row of guards.

The gate slammed shut with an ominous thud that made Pearly almost jump out of her skin.

This was definitely not a walk in the park.

CHAPTER 8

The Woe family was marched into a small hut perched on four skinny stilts at the perimeter of the compound. Their knives and ropes had been confiscated and three guards stood outside. No one spoke to them. No one told them what was going on. They were simply herded up the ramp and left there.

Hopefully not to rot, thought Pearly. Which probably wouldn't take very long in the heat and humidity of this peculiar little valley. *They could be pickled in an afternoon! Skeletons in days.*

Inside the hut, the air was thick, not just with humidity, but also with worry. And it wasn't only Pearly who was worrying. It was the entire Woe family – even Pig! Which of course made Pearly's worries flap their wings ever more frantically.

Pig lay in one corner of the hut, his snout resting on his trotters. *Something is desperately wrong with Ma*, he oink-whimpered. *My snout aches with it.*

Pearly stroked the fine white hairs along his back. She wished she knew how to help him.

Angel and Ricky leant up against each other in another corner, sweat trickling down their faces, their water bottles nestled in their laps. Pearly really felt for them. Her father had been planning this adventure for years and had come up with a solid new theory as to the location of the ancient city of Mu Savan. The city was a big part of Anachakan folklore and beliefs, but there had been no real evidence that it ever actually existed. Until recently. Back in his study in Woe Mansion, Ricky had been as excited as a toddler at a playground. He couldn't wait for the trip to start to test out the new information provided by the aerial laser scanning of the area. And now it seemed likely he wouldn't be able to prove his theory. No wonder he was so prickly and huffy earlier. Now Angel and Ricky stared into space, took swigs from their water bottles and sighed in unison.

And poor Grandpa Woe – Pearly couldn't bear to make eye contact with him. His distress was etched into every wrinkle around his eyes and right across his weather-beaten face.

Grandpa Woe worried for Ban Noa.

He worried for the villagers.

He worried for his friend King Alung Chu.

He paced up and down the small space they were

being held in. Every now and then, he stood at the window and shouted at the guards to take them to the new king – King Foom Chu. Grandpa Woe was not a shouter, so this made everything seem all the more desperate to Pearly.

The sun was quite low in the sky now – already hidden behind the jagged peaks to the west on the other side of the Mekong River. *Why did they need to be guarded?* Pearly wondered. *Why did they need to be held this way? They weren't enemies.* The Woes were long-time friends of the people of Ban Noa.

Grandpa Woe leant out the window and tried to reason with the guard standing closest to him. "I am sure," he said in a conciliatory tone, "that King Foom Chu would be happy to see me. I have known him since he was a youngster. I took him caving with me when he was a young man. We are friends. We are not threats."

Pearly was impressed with Grandpa Woe's command of the language. He almost sounded like a local. She leant out of the other window space and watched. No matter what Grandpa Woe said, the guards didn't flinch. Didn't move a muscle. They reminded Pearly of the royal guards at Buckingham Palace in their enormous black furry hats and red uniforms. These Ban Noa guards weren't in uniform – they wore colourful sarongs and loose-fitting shirts – but they were similarly disciplined and trained. Pearly had tried to distract one of the royal guards on their trip to London when she was five, but she couldn't even make him blink. Grandpa Woe was having the same difficulty now.

Grandpa Woe cursed under his breath and then flopped down onto the rattan flooring, sighing with defeat.

"Your instincts about this place were on the money, Angel," he said, his head hanging. "There is something so very wrong here."

Pig lifted his head off his trotters and squealed loudly. Grandpa Woe chuckled. "And, yes, you were right too, Pig. There is trouble here. I just wished I knew what kind."

Ricky moved to sit beside his father. "I agree. It's preposterous that we're being held prisoner. Utterly ridiculous. This has never happened before. And there are so many questions to be answered. Why did they move the village? What happened to King Alung Chu? Ban Noa never needed guards before. The people of Anachak kept to themselves, didn't interfere with the river trade – rarely even left this mountainside. What has changed?"

"Maybe one of the neighbouring countries has taken an interest in the kingdom and is causing trouble?" offered Angel. "I have often wondered how Anachak has remained untouched by the outside world for so long. It was really just a matter of time."

"Whatever has happened," said Grandpa Woe, "it's heartbreaking."

Pearly listened to the conversation with growing unease, muttering *smoky bacon* in English, in Pig, in Italian under her breath, over and over. Even though she had wanted this adventure to go smoothly, she had expected challenges, but she had not expected to become a prisoner, stuck in a hut, in the middle of the Anachakan jungle. She draped her arm over Pig. She felt for him. He was so close to being reunited with his ma, yet so far at the same time.

Just then, there was movement outside. Footsteps on the ramp. Two guards entered and instructed the Woes to follow them outside.

Relief and alarm shot through Pearly. It was wonderful to be leaving their bamboo prison finally, but where were the guards taking them?

Pearly sensed more trouble ahead. And she didn't need Pig's snout to tell her so.

CHAPTER 9

Pearly's knees trembled as she followed the guards down the ramp and into the compound. Scattered around were several small huts like the one they had just been in. Massive carved statues of the Divine Sow dotted the orange dirt of the courtyard in front of a large wooden building that stretched across the back of the compound. The building sat low to the ground, rather than on stilts, and it seemed to butt up against several mossy pillars that towered behind it. And it was huge. Its roof had a steep pitch, the gable adorned with wooden panels, intricately carved with images of pigs. And strangely, although pigs were depicted everywhere throughout the compound, there were no actual pigs, except for Pig, anywhere to be seen. Pearly had not seen a single pig in the compound since they arrived. She could hear them though – their squeals and grunts and oinks soaring over the fence from the village.

The guards herded the family towards the large building, which Pearly assumed was the king's residence. They stopped in front of a raised platform with a piggy-carved rooftop and bamboo railings all around. A door opened and a man emerged. He wore a jungle green sarong and white long-sleeved shirt, flecked with gold. A rich purple sash stretched around a large belly, and a matching sash wound around his forehead. Pearly was sure this man was the new king. She didn't like the look of him. Something about him made her stomach slosh and bubble. Perhaps it was the way his eyes narrowed as he looked at them? Or maybe how he thrust his chin forwards, his mouth downturned into a sneer? Or was it the enormous spear he held at his side? She wasn't sure, but she knew Pig felt it too, because he rubbed his ribs against her calves and oinked softly, OINKY OINKY NO-NO! OINKY OINKY NO-NO! *Trouble, I smell trouble.* Two younger men followed close behind the king and stood on either side of him. One looked scruffy and had a long beard hanging from his chin, the other was muscly and strong and had a determined glint in his eye and a sneering mouth, like the king's.

"Foom Chu!" Grandpa Woe cried, relief in his voice. He broke from their line and approached the platform, only to be pushed back by the pointy end of numerous spears.

"*King* Foom Chu," the king replied, his voice as gruff and unwelcoming as his face.

Grandpa Woe bowed his head. "I am sorry. King Foom Chu, I am so pleased to see you. And also, you Tub." Grandpa Woe nodded at the strong-looking man to the king's left, who screwed his face with annoyance at Grandpa Woe. "I mean, Prince Tub Chu. Of course," Grandpa Woe corrected. "And Prince Vam Chu." He dipped his head to the bearded man, then held his arms out, palms up. "I think there has been a misunderstanding. We have been held prisoner."

King Foom Chu tapped the end of his spear on the platform floor. "There is no misunderstanding. You have no permission to be here. You are trespassing on Anachakan land."

Grandpa Woe laughed, though Pearly noted it was high-pitched and squeaky. "We are friends, King Foom Chu. You must remember me – Gordon Woe. I took you–"

"I know who you are," King Foom Chu interrupted. "But Anachak is different now. I am the king. And Tub and Vam are now my princes, their sisters my princesses. You will show respect." The way this new king was speaking to Grandpa Woe made Pearly shift from foot to foot.

"Yes. I can see that," Grandpa Woe said slowly, cautiously choosing his words. "What happened to King Alung Chu?" he asked finally.

52

"Gone," stated King Foom Chu, and thrust his chubby chin out even further.

"Gone?" Grandpa Woe repeated. "Alung would not *go* – he loves Anachak."

"Swallowed," stated King Foom Chu.

Swallowed? Pearly gulped as she imagined the king being slowly swallowed by a giant anaconda, the anaconda's body changing shape as the king's body moved deeper inside it. She shook her head free of the image, reminding herself there were no anacondas in this part of the world. Well, she hoped there wasn't, anyhow.

"Swallowed?" Pearly's father turned his head to one side, his eyebrows scrunched together. "Swallowed? How?" Ricky's Anachakan wasn't as fluent as Grandpa's or Pearly's, but he seemed to get the message across.

"Swallowed by the jungle. Princess Jong and Prince Keej too. That is why the kingdom is now mine."

Ricky's face paled. "I am not sure that it is possible ... for the jungle to ... swallow people." His words faltered as he struggled to find the right words.

"It is true. The Divine Sow is displeased. It is her will."

"I am confused," Grandpa Woe said. "How has the Divine Sow caused the jungle to swallow the royal family?"

What are they saying? Pig oinked softly beside Pearly.

"The king said the Divine Sow is unhappy–" Pearly whispered.

Pig squealed at the mention of the Divine Sow, and the king levelled his eyes at him, as if he saw him for the first time. "Why is that pig in my compound?" he demanded.

Pig squealed and trotted around in an agitated circle.

"Pig is ... Pig is ..." Angel tried, but stopped, frustrated, unable to find the right words in Anachakan.

"Pig is the son of the Divine Sow," Pearly took over for her mother. "He is worried that she is unhappy."

The king snorted, and glanced at his sons, who snort-laughed back. What was so funny? "Ah! *That* pig!" the king said, throwing back his head and laughing some more. "I recall my brother sending off the old sow's precious baby son. It was a mistake. Typical."

Pearly's skin prickled. She did not like the sound of this.

"But that is not the sow I speak of. She is the current living sow – though for how long, we don't know." Pearly gasped. She glanced down at Pig and hoped he couldn't work out what the king was saying. "She is only a descendant of the original and most holy Divine Sow, she is not the *Divine* Sow. Another foolish mistake from my brother. A myth. The Divine Sow is the Sacred Statue–"

54

"Yes!" Ricky exclaimed. "The Sacred Statue of the Divine Sow. We know all about it. It is housed in the lost city of Mu Savan."

Prince Tub Chu gasped. "You know about Mu Savan?" he challenged, sounding displeased, pinning Pearly's father with fierce eyes.

Ricky didn't seem to pick up on the prince's displeasure and he continued on enthusiastically, despite Angel elbowing him. "Indeed," he said. "That, in fact, is why we are here. I have been studying Mu Savan for many years. I have searched these jungles twice for it, but now I have new evidence and ... I think I know where it is. King Alung Chu gave his permission for us to come at any time to search for it." Ricky's enthusiasm was mountaintop high and, to Pearly's horror, he seemed oblivious to the thunderous expression that was taking over the king's face.

"You have no such permission from me," the king shouted, the shock of it making Ricky take a step backwards. "The Sacred Statue of the Divine Sow is no business of yours. She is already displeased. The earth has been shaking. The rains have come early. The river floods are far too frequent. The jungle is swallowing anyone who travels too far from Ban Noa. The Balance has been disturbed. The current living sow is old and weak, and she has not produced a new sow for a very long time. The lineage is likely to be broken, and this will disturb the Balance even more. And the people of Ban Noa are afraid. As they should be. It is a difficult time for Anachak. A time of change."

Pearly crouched low and hugged Pig tight, his little heart thumping his ribcage. She didn't know how much he understood, but it was enough to make him distressed. She watched as her parents and grandfather looked at one another anxiously.

Grandpa Woe's face was ashen. He stood regarding the king for a long moment, his tongue sliding over his teeth, his lips smacking together, as he considered the king's words. "King Foom Chu," he said, his voice soft and oozing respect. "I am deeply troubled that the people of Ban Noa have suffered so much and I am very much saddened by the news. King Alung Chu, as you know, was a great friend of mine. I ask permission to find answers to his disappearance."

"Are your ears not working, old man?" King Foom Chu sneered. "There are no answers to be found. Alung is gone. It is the will of the Sacred Statue of the Divine Sow. And it is the will of the new king for you all to be held until my guards can escort you to the river and ensure you leave. Your presence will only disturb the Balance further." The king waved at his guards. "Take them away. Guard them throughout the night. And get that pig out of this compound. Now!"

CHAPTER 10

As soon as the sun had dropped behind the mountain peaks, Grandpa Woe led Pearly away from the window where she had been keeping a lookout since Pig was thrown out of the compound and the Woes imprisoned once more.

"Don't worry. We'll find him tomorrow, sweetheart," he said as he wrapped her in a tight Grandpa Woe hug. Pearly loved her grandfather's hugs – they weren't given very often, but they were always there when she needed them, like tonight.

The Woes closed the bamboo shutters to the window openings. Grandpa Woe lit a camping lamp, Angel a mosquito coil. Ricky set up the tiny cooking burner and boiled water for their dehydrated meals. Pearly selected the sachets and opened each carefully so Ricky could pour in the hot water, once boiled. Her heart skipped a beat when she spied Pig's oat and vegie mix pack. She shoved it under a rolled-up tarp out of view.

Hopefully, Pig was with his ma and cousins and they were sharing their food.

Pearly picked at her Mexican chilli and rice. She had only had a couple of bananas since breakfast, and had expended more energy in one day of jungle trekking than she would usually expend in a week at Woe Mansion, even counting her morning jogs with Ricky and her physical training with Angel, but she was far too anxious to eat.

Once they had packed everything away, Ricky stretched out his map in the middle of them, smoothing out the folds and crinkles. He sat cross-legged with pencil and notebook poised. He was keen to devise a plan.

"It's simple," Grandpa Woe whispered. He was speaking in English, but regardless seemed he didn't want the guards or anyone else to hear. "We have to stay. That's all there is to it. There is something very wrong with this new Ban Noa." He raised his head, looked towards the closed door and lowered his voice further. "You can't deny it. We must not leave tomorrow. Stage a sit-in – refuse to move, whatever it takes. If that doesn't work, then we will have to pretend to leave by boat, then sneak back in."

"Father, I simply can't go along with your plan." Ricky's voice was soft and calm, but Pearly could tell by the way he fidgeted with the corner of his notebook that he was far from calm. "It is an important part of the Guild's charter and rules to respect the wishes of the people of the land we adventure on," he continued. "So we have no choice but to call the expedition off. As much as it pains me, after all my planning and study, it is the only way. Besides, it's getting far too dangerous to continue." He glanced at Pearly as he said this. Pearly's stomach knotted. Was he calling it off because of her?

"You can't be serious, lad." Grandpa Woe's whisper had grown into a fierce hiss. "I owe it King Alung Chu to find out what's going on. Alung was more than a friend – he saved my life, rescued me from the cave I was trapped in, and then with the help of the village nursed me back to good health." He thumped his fist on the floor.

Pearly's parents exchanged concerned glances, their faces glowing eerily in the flickering lamplight.

"But father, the charter ..." Ricky countered.

Grandpa Woe brushed off an insect feasting on his hairy knees. "I don't care what the charter says!" This was beyond shocking as Grandpa Woe was the one who wrote the charter, rules and guidelines in the first place. "I am not leaving until I find out what has happened to Alung and his family. I don't buy a word of what Foom says, not one word."

Angel rested her hand gently on Grandpa Woe's shoulder. "I understand how you feel, Gordon, but as

59

much as I don't like it, I think Ricky has a point. We are the Woe family. You are the founder of the Guild. Surely, we have no choice. We don't have permission to continue. The only thing we need to work out now, I think, is how to persuade the king to return our machetes, knives and ropes and find Pig, of course. We must work out a rescue plan. Then tomorrow we just have to leave."

Pearly was grateful for the Pig Rescue Plan – the whole time her family had been arguing she had wanted to shout, *But what about Pig? What if the jungle has swallowed him?* Now, she was surprised that they were so ready to give in. This was not at all how her parents had recounted their adventures to Pearly over the years. Pearly had always admired their courage and resolve. They always seemed to find clever ways out of sticky situations like this. They never just retreated. Somehow, she felt that her parents were using the Guild's charter to back out, to slink away and, sadly, she was starting to believe it was all because of her.

Pearly held her legs tight against her chest and willed herself not to cry.

When it was clear that no agreement could be reached, the adults huffed off to their separate corners to sleep. They were all too moody to notice that Pearly was still wide awake and propped up against the wall, waiting for someone to ask her what she thought.

That was when the earth began to rumble. Softly at first, then louder and louder – a grumbly rumble coming from deep below, making the floor vibrate. Pearly sat up straight, alert, her ears cocked. Was she imagining it?

Obviously not, because one by one, her grumpy family sat up, frowning, palms to the floor feeling the vibrations rise through the floor.

"Is it an earthquake?" Pearly asked.

"Don't think so," said Angel. "I've suffered through many earthquakes growing up in Iceland. This feels too consistent."

"Agreed. I was here during an earthquake and after tremors in '97," said Grandpa Woe. "The whole place shook and rattled. Nothing like this."

"This must be the earth grumbling Foom Chu was talking about. It almost sounds mechanical," said Ricky.

"Like the earthmovers when you built that cellar, Grandpa Woe," added Pearly.

"Yes, it does a bit," Grandpa Woe agreed. "But that's not possible here. They don't have that sort of equipment and it is underneath us, so doubly impossible. Strange. No wonder the villagers are afraid."

The rumbling continued for an hour or more – and it was certainly frightening. Mainly because there was no logical explanation for it. Could the Sacred Statue of the Divine Sow really make the earth grumble? It sounded preposterous, but what else could it be? The whole notion made Pearly's shoulders knot and her mind conjure up other possibilities. *Perhaps the village had been built on the top of a volcano ready to explode? Or maybe they were perched on the lair of a Godzilla-sized centipede trying to scratch its way out. Or a nest of thousands of raptor eggs hatching?*

Mamma mia! She had to stop these thoughts.

Eventually, all was silent again and the Woes crept back to their corners to try to get some sleep.

But as soon as Pearly closed her eyes, her mind swept past the images of what had made the rumbling and back to images of Pig being thrown out of the compound, legs kicking. His squealing distress rang in her ears and her heart fluttered within her chest. She felt bereft without him. Sleep was going to be impossible. She was just turning over when she heard movement to her left. She opened one eye to see her mother wiggle across to her father and shake him awake. "What has got into you?" she whispered. "Why are you so willing to desert the people of Ban Noa?"

Her father ran his hand over his face. "We have to go. She's our only daughter ..." Pearly couldn't catch what her father whispered next, just the odd word here and there. "... isn't ready ... we wouldn't be in this

position if ... those monkeys ... worries ... all in danger."
It wasn't difficult to fill in the gaps. Those odd words
told her everything she needed to know.

Her mother sighed. "I worry too. And I agree, it's
becoming dangerous."

Pearly curled herself into a tight ball to stop herself
from shaking. Great sobs rose into her throat. She
pushed them down only to have them cling tight to one
another and form a great ball of hurt – and shame –
deep in her gut.

Her worst fears were confirmed.

Her parents wanted to leave because of her. She
had ruined the adventure.

She had failed yet again.

She would never be an Adventurologist.

CHAPTER 11

Pearly was bone stiff and heart sore when she woke the next morning. She propped herself up against the wall of the hut, the sun slanting in through the gaps around the window opening opposite her. Thankfully, her family were still asleep. She didn't want to face them yet. How could she look her parents in the eye when she knew that she was such a disappointment – a burden – and now, because of her, they had to cut their adventure short, her father's dream of finding Mu Savan would be extinguished and the problems of the people of Ban Noa ignored? Had she really held them back? She hadn't complained. She had cut that path through the jungle like the others. She had communicated with the monkeys. How was their predicament her fault? If only Pig was here to talk to.

Pig.

Pearly shuddered.

Where is he now? she fretted. *What if they were*

escorted out of Ban Noa without Pig? What if the jungle swallowed him like it swallowed King Alung Chu? She couldn't bear being separated from him. She pushed herself to her feet, threw open the shutters and peered out of the window. Two guards were standing on either side of the ramp, their spear tops glistening in the morning sunlight.

Grandpa Woe yawned and stretched and scratched his stubbly chin. He joined Pearly at the window. "Can you hear him?" he asked.

Pearly smiled a sad smile. "I've been trying. I can hear lots of pigs, but I can't make out Pig's voice above the rest. Oh, Grandpa Woe, what's happened to him? If he was allowed to roam freely with his cousins, he would be at the fence oinking a message to me. But I've heard nothing."

"Don't underestimate Pig. He's extraordinary," said Grandpa Woe. "Perhaps he's with his ma. The king said she was *sow* poorly ..." Pearly rolled her eyes at Grandpa Woe's attempt to jolly her.

There was some groaning behind them as Angel, then Ricky stirred and sat up. Pearly's eyes welled. She didn't know if she felt ashamed or angry or betrayed. They really hadn't given her a proper chance.

Ricky coughed and blew his nose. Her usually neat as a pin father was disturbingly crumpled – his hair an untidy bird's nest. It didn't suit him.

Angel ran her fingers through her long red curls, dragged her adventure pack to her and pulled out a banana. "Lucky they didn't take our packs – otherwise we'd starve, or die of thirst. Would it hurt them to give us some fresh water? Or to come and empty that stinky bucket? No, it wouldn't. It's one thing to be held captive, but it is another to be ignored like this." Angel pulled down the leaves of banana peel angrily. She was in a bad mood. She was just about to take a bite, when there was a sudden whoosh and a frantic scramble and she was knocked to the ground, banana-less.

The family gawked at Angel in shock, as a cheeky little macaque monkey swung across the rafters, clutching the banana.

Arr-arr-ooo-ooo, arr-arr-ooo-ooo! Arr-arr-ooo-ooo, arr-arr-ooo-ooo! He squawked and laughed and hung from one arm.

"Wah-Wah!" Pearly exclaimed. She chittered at Wah-Wah, telling him he was too bold for his own good. *Where have you been?* she asked, tilting her head from side to side in question.

Hiding, Wah-Wah answered, as he slid down from the rafters and perched on Pearly's shoulder, chittering constantly and gobbling Angel's banana. *Monkeys not allowed in village, banana head.* He vaulted to the ground, slid his lips back and grinned a monkey-toothed grin at the circle of stunned faces around him.

Grandpa Woe huddled close to Pearly and whispered in her ear. "Ask him if he knows about the jungle swallowing King Alung Chu and the prince and princess."

Pearly opened her eyes wide. That would not be easy. And what was the point? Her parents were going to march them out of here, without a second thought about the old king. Regardless, she took in a long breath and rehearsed in her mind how best to convey Grandpa Woe's question. She sat on the floor beside Wah-Wah and made noises and gestures to ask about the royal family.

Wah-Wah listened intently, then shrugged, a very human shrug. *Don't know*, he chittered. *King is gone, but jungle doesn't like the taste of people.*

Well, that's what Pearly thought he said. She relayed the message to the rest of the family.

Grandpa Woe slumped beside Pearly, chewing his bottom lip and rubbing his stubble.

Angel crouched to join the group. "Ask him if he knows where Pig is," she said. "We didn't get far with the Rescue Pig Plan last night."

No, thought Pearly grimly. *Too busy working out why I shouldn't be here.*

Pearly approached Wah-Wah, who was now sitting on top of Grandpa Woe's pack. *Pig?* she said, and oinked and snorted in a piggy way to make sure she was getting her message across. *Do you know where Pig is?*

Wah-Wah jumped up and down on the pack and thumped his palms against its sides. *Yes! I have a message for banana head from Pig.*

What message?

Wah-Wah is too hungry. Need banana. The little monkey flopped onto its side, looking forlorn.

"Bananas!" Pearly called to her parents. "He won't talk without bananas."

"That was my last," said Angel as she rummaged in her pack for something else.

"Here," said Ricky, holding up a rather squishy overripe banana.

Wah-Wah snatched the banana from Ricky's hands and gobbled it in seconds.

Still hungry, he complained.

Message first, insisted Pearly.

O-kay. The little monkey crawled into Pearly's lap and snuggled against her shoulder. Pearly stroked his back. He smelt earthy like the jungle floor and his breath wafted bananas. She tickled under his chin and encouraged him to talk. Wah-Wah chittered softly, and said words to the effect, *Pig's mama is very sick. He will not leave until she is better.*

Pearly translated the message back to her family.

Ricky thumped his head with the heel of his hand.

Angel let out an enormous sigh.

Grandpa Woe smiled smugly. "So it's settled then," he said. "We're staying. The monkey – and Pig – have spoken."

Pearly wasn't sure if she was relieved or disappointed. Heck, she didn't know how to feel any more. The adventure had taken a strange and dangerous turn, and that danger made Pearly's stomach churn as if she had just gulped down three caramel milkshakes followed by a dozen hot dogs with mustard. But knowing that her father wanted to leave because of her made her feel a whole lot worse.

Now, more than ever, she needed to prove herself to her parents.

She hoped she was ready.

She had to be.

CHAPTER 12

The Woes didn't have even a minute to argue about their plans.

Outside the hut a crowd was gathering. Wah-Wah fled through a side window. The gates had been opened and Pearly could see dozens of pigs, tails wagging, milling about the open gate. She frantically searched for Pig, but he was nowhere to be seen. None of the pigs ventured through the gates, but a long stream of villagers filed through and gathered around the raised platform the king had stood at yesterday.

"Look at them," said Grandpa Woe, turning imploring eyes to Pearly's parents. "Look at their faces. They are full of fear. Sad. And so silent. This is not like the Anachakan people at all. They are noisy, happy people. Friendly. We have to help them."

Pearly could see what Grandpa Woe meant. It was such a forlorn procession. *What's making them so afraid?* Pearly wondered. That rumbling last night certainly made Pearly feel afraid. *Could that be it? Or was it something more?*

Pearly's parents remained closed lipped. But Pearly could read their faces, and she knew that deep down they were worried about the villagers too – but not worried enough to stay and help them, apparently. Not with Pearly around anyhow.

The Woes were escorted out of their hut, through the crowd, which parted noiselessly to let them pass. They were told to stand in a line beside the king's platform, facing the villagers.

Pearly's fingers trembled at her sides. She chewed her bottom lip. She felt Pig's absence sorely. She longed for him to rub his ribs against her legs, to whisper, *Smoky bacon to those worries.* She murmured the piggy cursing under her breath, stood on tippy-toes and stretched her neck, hoping that she would glimpse Pig among the pigs still bunching around the open gate.

No Pig, but she did catch a moment pass between her parents. Ricky slipped his hand into Angel's, gave it a squeeze, and then whispered, "I feel sick. What have we done? She should never have come."

Pearly leant out of the way before her father spotted her. She recognised the anguish in his voice. She knew that her worries often jumbled her thoughts and made it difficult for her to be the right kind of brave to be a worthy Adventurologist, but she never thought being on an adventure would cause so much worry for her father. She hung her head. Ricky saw her as a hindrance, not a future Adventurologist. She would never pass his test – she would never be an Adventurologist in her father's eyes.

The door to the king's residence opened and King Foom Chu and his sons strutted out, just as they had yesterday. Today the king wore a much more elaborate belt, sash and head scarf – sunset red, with golden pigs woven into the fabric. He thrust out his chin and surveyed the crowd.

Pearly looked at the faces of the people in front of her. There was no joy anywhere to be found in this new Ban Noa. No wonder Grandpa Woe was taking it so badly.

The king tapped the end of his spear three times to get everyone's attention, which was totally unnecessary as the crowd were as silent as monks on a cliff top retreat. He cleared his throat before he spoke. "People of Anachak. The Sacred Statue of the Divine Sow is displeased. Last night, the earth grumbled again – grumbled a warning, reminding us that the Balance has been disturbed. These foreigners have trespassed on our land and are disturbing the Balance. King Foom Chu is here to protect you. He is here to make the Sacred Statue of the Divine Sow happy again and to restore the Balance and–"

"Ah, er, King Foom Chu ..." Grandpa Woe interrupted. He took off his orange hat, held it against his stomach and took a tentative step towards the platform. Pearly's stomach flip-flopped. What was he doing? "Ah ... about that ... may I make a suggestion?"

The king fixed Grandpa Woe with his narrow-eyed stare and his chubby chin raise, but his lips remained clamped.

Grandpa fiddled with his hat nervously, then continued. "We heard the earth grumbling last night. It was very strange. But it made me think about the Sacred Statue of the Divine Sow and the Balance. Perhaps the earth's shaking has toppled the statue. It is certainly a possibility. If you allow us to continue on our expedition, I am sure that we will be able to find Mu Savan and the Sacred Statue and we may be able to return it to its rightful place and perhaps restore the Balance."

Grandpa Woe is so clever, Pearly thought as she watched the crowd. They were hanging on his every word. Nearby, she noticed a woman with a young child on her hip, curl her mouth into a smile. The man beside her had his hands on his chest; he leaned in towards Grandpa Woe. The change in the crowd was palpable. Was it hope that Pearly saw flickering in their eyes, in their shoulders, their stance? She couldn't be sure, but whatever it was, it was literally spreading through the crowd.

The king remained stony faced, unaffected by Grandpa Woe's words.

"I am worried for your people," Grandpa Woe continued. "I think we could help–"

"NO!" shouted the king, and the whole crowd winced, their hope snapped from them. "The jungle is swallowing people! *You* must leave. *You* must leave now! *You* are causing the Balance to be disturbed. *You* are displeasing the Sacred Statue of the Divine Sow." King Foom Chu waved his spear at the crowd, egging them on to agree with him. "Leave now!"

The princes joined in the chant, then a few people at the front. "Leave! Leave now!" The voices swelled as others joined in. "Leave. Leave now!"

Pearly covered her face with her hands and watched through her fingers. The chant was getting louder and louder. It echoed all around the compound. It should have been terrifying, threatening. But Pearly soon realised it was neither. She took her hands from her face. The chant was loud, but there was no passion, no real feeling or anger or commitment in it. It was automatic – the crowd was just doing as they were told, like they were hypnotised or something.

This was so horrible to watch.

Orribile. (Italian.) *Na yanyan.* (Anachakan.) *Oinky-squio.* (Pig.) *Ahh-ooo-ooo-ooo.* (Macaque.)

Anger bubbled inside Pearly. They couldn't possibly leave now. They had to work out what was wrong with Ban Noa and Anachak. They had to do something for these people.

"What are you all afraid of?" Pearly wondered out loud, at the precise moment the king lowered his spear and the chant ceased. Her words were softly spoken, meant only for her own ears, but they boomed across the now silent compound.

"What did you say?" bellowed the king.

Pearly gulped. Her eyes flicked from side to side.

"Come here and repeat what you just said – this time, to my face!" the king ordered. He shook his head, patting his belly and chuckling in a smug way that made Pearly feel hot and humiliated.

Pearly looked to Angel and Ricky. Ricky appeared as if he might drop to the ground in a dead faint. Angel pushed her red curls behind her ears. She was red-faced and sweaty, but she nodded her head in encouragement at Pearly.

Pearly stepped towards the king, her feet like bricks in her boots.

"I ... I ... just wondered what you are afraid of, King Foom Chu." It wasn't exactly what she said, but the words just flew off her tongue and, as she was saying them, she felt as if her tongue knew best, because this is what was needed to be said. "Why are you afraid of letting my family look for Mu Savan?"

"Pearly!" Ricky jumped out from the line, slapped his hand over her mouth, and pulled her next to him, holding her close to his side. "She is a mere child, King Foom Chu. She doesn't know what she is saying."

Pearly wiggled free. "I do know what I'm saying. The king is afraid of us finding Mu Savan!"

The king's belly swelled as he drew in a deep breath, the red and gold band stretching across his middle, fit to burst, his face drawn into a weird smirk as his eyes swept from Pearly to the crowd, who all seemed to be holding their collective breath, eyes wide, waiting for the king's response.

Rivers of sweat ran down Pearly's back. Her knees knocked together.

What had she done?

CHAPTER 13

"King Foom Chu is not afraid." The king's hot breath almost knocked Pearly over.

Then he burst out laughing – a raucous, ridiculous laugh that had him bending over and holding his hands across his large belly. The princes on either side of him laughed too. Prince Tub Chu's permanent sneer turned itself upside down. He seemed to find it all so hilarious that he slapped his father on the back, hissing like a snake.

It was such a strange reaction, Pearly had no idea how to react herself. What was funny? Was he mocking her? She had no idea.

"King Foom Chu is afraid of nothing," he said eventually, wiping the laughter tears from his eyes. "If you want to get swallowed by the jungle – go ahead. Go search for Mu Savan. Go find the Sacred Statue. But don't return until you have restored the Balance and pleased the Divine Sow!"

"Thank you! Thank you!" Grandpa Woe said, palms together, bowing deeply, over and over.

"Ah, but Father, what if we can't–" stuttered Ricky.

"We will do our very best," cut in Grandpa Woe, still bowing, "and we will report our findings back to you on our return."

The king spread his hand across his chin. He cast his eyes across the crowd, a sneaky not-to-be-trusted smile crawling across his face. "And if I am not happy with what you have accomplished, the pig must stay in Ban Noa. He will be your payment."

The blood drained from Pearly's face. Grandpa Woe took her hand and then eyeballed her stunned parents. "Come on," he urged, and led them through the shocked crowd. "We will save you," he whispered in Anachakan to the bowed heads of the people, too afraid to make eye contact, as he pushed through them. "Trust us. We will save you."

Grandpa Woe led the family up the ramp into their prison hut to collect their packs. But once inside, he swiftly closed all the shutters. The family stood shaking in the middle of the dim, stuffy room.

"This is beyond foolish!" Ricky exploded. "What were you thinking, Father? We can't guarantee that we can restore the Balance – especially as I don't even believe that there is anything wrong with the Balance in the first place. I don't even believe in it at all, come to think of it - not in the way King Foom Chu means it. He's not speaking about the balance of nature, like in the *RAG*. He's talking about something else entirely! What if we don't find Mu Savan? I don't even know where it is now. Heck, I don't even know where *we* are!" He fell to his knees and rummaged through his adventure pack, pulled out the map and fumbled it open on the floor.

Angel slid her arm over Pearly's shoulder and rubbed her hand up and down her arm. "Don't worry, sweetheart. Your father is just worried for our safety, so he seems to be panicking a bit."

So am I, thought Pearly. But she didn't say so. Instead, she broke free from Angel and approached Grandpa Woe who was hovering over her father as he tried to pinpoint their location on one of his maps.

"What about Pig?" she said, blinking back tears. She didn't want to cry. She wanted to be strong. She wanted to show that she was worthy of being part of the adventure but worry about Pig was tearing her apart.

"Pig will be fine," Grandpa Woe said and drew her into a hug. "We will not leave Ban Noa without him. Do you trust me?"

Pearly nodded grimly. She trusted Grandpa Woe, but in her heart of hearts she wasn't sure that she believed him. How could he be so sure?

Grandpa Woe crouched beside Ricky who was on his hands and knees, tracing his finger over the map, mumbling. Angel and Pearly sat cross-legged close by. "We set off here," Ricky said, pointing. "There's the old Ban Noa. Then we headed towards Elephant Nose peak, until that monkey sent us in this direction ... for maybe an hour. Maybe two or three kays ..." He jumped up and went to the window and stuck his head out. "Can't see Elephant Nose from here, so we must have crossed into the next valley ... oh, look, here are markings that look very much like the rocky structures. This is where we are, I reckon." Grandpa leant in for a closer look. Ricky reached into his pack and produced a printout of a recent map showing the aerial laser scanning of the area.

Ricky flipped back and forth from the ancient map to his recent one. "Holy moly!" he said, as he checked again, and dropped back to his knees. "We are on the doorstep. Right on the doorstep! The laser scanning showed evidence of ruins only a few kays from here, north-east towards those limestone peaks. Maybe even closer."

Pearly felt a small bubble of excitement tickle her stomach. Maybe Grandpa Woe was right, maybe they could find the lost city. Maybe Pig could be rescued.

Grandpa Woe and Angel examined the maps closely.

"Father, was this where you went caving?" Ricky asked.

"No, lad. I explored the cave systems to the south of the peaks and on the other side of the ridge. I know I've been past this valley, though, as I remember seeing the weird fingers of rock – the ones all around the village. They were consumed by the jungle back then, tangled in vines and tree roots, sometimes almost part of a whole tree – the Anachakans have done a fair amount of clearing to build this new village. Then I must have headed south to the caves."

"We are so close. This is just fabulous." Ricky tipped the contents of his adventure pack onto the floor, his excitement seemingly overrunning his panic. "We must take stock of our supplies and ..."

"And get our equipment back. We can't go into that jungle without our machetes and rope and knives ..." Angel started sorting through her pack also.

Grandpa Woe slid back and leant against the far wall.

"Aren't you going to check your pack?" Angel asked. "If we hurry, we can make good ground before it gets dark."

"No need," Grandpa Woe said.

Angel and Ricky stopped what they were doing and frowned at him.

"Why?" they asked together.

"I'm not going."

Ricky rolled his eyes and plopped onto his backside. "You're not going! You were the one who insisted we stay and continue and now you say you're not going?"

"I never said I was going to continue on the expedition; I always said I was staying. I only went on about restoring the Balance and so forth to persuade the king. Which I might add didn't work – it was our brave Pearly that persuaded – or guilted him into agreeing." Pearly's face flushed at being called "brave". That was a word rarely used in the same sentence as her name. "I am staying put, so I can try to find out what is going on with the villagers. Snoop around. Try to talk to some of the people I know from the old days. I don't trust Foom Chu, and I won't be able to help Ban Noa if I am clambering about the jungle searching for lost ruins. That's your thing, lad, not mine. And it will make for an excellent distraction, while I get on with the real work. Remember, *knowledge is power*. Number 10 in 'Surviving Sticky Situations'."

"I guess that makes sense," said Angel. "But Foom Chu might not want you around."

"Don't worry. I'll feign an injury. Or I'll say I've been charged to stay and look after Pig. Foom Chu won't care about an old man being left behind."

"Or a young girl," added Ricky.

Pearly's arms tingled. "What do you mean?"

"You are staying too. I've decided. It will show Foom Chu we are serious about the expedition. That we don't want to be slowed down or ..."

"Burdened? By a useless ten-year-old who you wished you didn't bring? The mere child. Your big mistake." Pearly's tongue ran away with itself again. But she couldn't help it. There was too much hurt inside her to stop it from wagging.

Ricky stared at her open-mouthed. Angel leant across and pulled her close. "You are not a burden," she soothed, stroking Pearly's hair. "You're a learner. This is your first real adventure, I know. But this adventure has become a lot more than finding the lost city of Mu Savan. It has taken an unexpected turn, and we need to adapt our strategies and play to our strengths. So I think your father is probably right, but not for the reasons you think. It makes Adventurologing sense for you to stay. It adds weight to Grandpa Woe's story because we can say that you're staying to look after him. And while we're gone, you can find Pig – we really need to come up with a plan about Pig, and you are the best one to do that. And while you are doing that, you can help Grandpa Woe see what's happening here. You can be our eyes and ears – our information gatherer. That is an important job on any adventure. Knowledge is power. We need you to do this, Pearly."

Pearly shrugged out of her mother's arms and plopped next to Grandpa Woe, her arms folded tight across her chest. She could hear the truth in her mother's words, but she could also sense the relief. The relief of not having to worry about having Pearly the expert worrier and failed Adventurologist-in-training, the learner adventurer tagging along and getting in the way.

CHAPTER 14

It took a good few hours before Angel and Ricky were ready to start out on their trek. Most of that time was spent on convincing King Foom Chu to allow Grandpa Woe and Pearly to stay in Ban Noa. He was not impressed – immediately suspicious and snively about it. Grandpa Woe had wrapped a bandage around his ankle and did a wonderful job of hobbling and wincing in pain, and eventually Foom Chu shouted at them to get out of his sight. He banished them from the compound and told them they would have to stay under one of the huts on the far edge of the village – as far away from him as possible. They were forbidden to speak to anyone, or to ask for food. They were on their own.

It was now after midday. And the Woes were standing on the jungle edge, eyeing the limestone peaks to the north-east.

"We should head off," Ricky said finally. "I hope to make it close to the area where I suspect Mu Savan may be hidden, probably swallowed by the jungle, no doubt."

Pearly jolted when her father used that word. Angel gave him a look.

But it was too late. King Foom Chu's words and warnings – *The Sacred Statue of the Divine Sow is displeased, and the jungle is swallowing anyone who ventures too far from Ban Noa* – chimed through Pearly's head and made her arms prickle.

She didn't really believe it was possible, but King Alung Chu and his son and daughter *were* missing – that was a fact. Could the jungle have swallowed them? The mere suggestion made her fear for her parents' safety.

"Group hug!" said her mother, and the Woes huddled together and held each other for a long moment.

Eventually, they broke apart and stood awkwardly looking at one another.

Angel stroked Pearly under her cheek. "We'll be fine," she said. "We have red strips that we'll attach to trees at every turn, so we can't get lost and so you can find us if you need to. We'll be back before you know it, and hopefully we will have news to please the king about Mu Savan and–"

"Time's marching on," Pearly's father interrupted. He put his arm across Pearly's shoulder. "I'm sorry I've been a bit strung out lately." He looked deep into her eyes. "Forgive me?"

Pearly gave a small nod. She did forgive him, but she didn't like it. She didn't want to be a worry, a burden. It made her feel as if she had gorilla hands pushing on her shoulders, weighing her down.

She resolved to find Pig swiftly and then to gather information. Surely, she could manage that! Knowledge is power and gaining that knowledge might just help to make her father worry less and maybe even trust her more.

"Good luck with Pig," said Angel. "Remember the pair of you are our eyes and ears. I hope you can work out what on earth is going on here."

"And I hope you two find that lost city," said Grandpa Woe. "That will make our departure a whole lot easier!"

Ricky and Angel pulled out their machetes and started carefully slashing through the foliage to create a way through. Grandpa Woe tugged on his hat and headed into the village. Pearly glimpsed her parents as they disappeared into the sea of green. Would she ever have the courage to step boldly into danger like that? Pearly looked into that jungle and saw tigers and snakes and jungle plants that gobbled up a king, a prince and a princess. That was who she was. No training would make her any different. She was kidding herself.

She hurried to catch up with Grandpa Woe.

"It's up to us now, Pearly," he said, pretend hobbling as he walked. "It's time you searched for Pig. And that's *snout* going to be easy!" Grandpa chuckled and winked at her. Pearly didn't appreciate the joke. "Come on, lighten up. It will all work out." He slung his arm over her shoulder as they walked to the last hut in the village. "I'm going to try to reacquaint myself with some of my old pals. Let's meet back here at this hut as soon as the sun dips behind the mountains, and we'll set up camp. Okay? Oh, and keep your pack with you. I don't trust that Foom Chu at all."

Pearly agreed. She hooked her hands around the straps of her adventure pack and strode off, resolving to lighten up as Grandpa Woe suggested. *First, I am going to find Pig*, she told herself. *That's the least I can do. Then together we are going to be super snoops and find out what this rottenness is all about!* The thought made her heart beat faster. *Somehow … Maybe …* she added. *Oh, mamma mia! Smoky bacon!* How on earth was she going to do this?

Wah-Wah had said that Pig was with his ma. So where would the Divine Sow – or "that old sow" as the king had called her – be? The village wasn't that big, so Pearly decided to be methodical and walk down each path between the huts. Surely, she would find him that way.

But a slow and careful walk up and down and across brought her no joy. Hens strutted and clucked. Pigs cavorted. Their trotters kicked up dust. Their squeaks and grunts and squeals were a constant soundtrack. She tried to ask some of them about Pig, but was quickly frustrated. They seemed to ignore her and when she stopped to listen to them, she found that she had difficulty understanding them. Their grunts and oinks didn't make a lot of sense to her.

Large groups of pigs sheltered in lazy groups under the shade of the huts or palm trees, snouts resting on trotters. She searched each group carefully. But there was no Pig and no Ma.

And no people either. Which only made the whole search even more alarming. This Ban Noa was not like any other place she had been to. It was eerie. And sad. Occasionally, she saw a head duck below a window opening. Often, she saw the shadow of someone slipping quickly inside before she got too close. It was obvious that the villagers had been forbidden to speak with her.

Pearly plodded on. The adventure pack was heavy against her back. Her limbs ached and her eyes itched. It was baking hot. She dropped her pack to the ground, pulled off her hat and plopped under the shade of a palm tree near one of the mossy fingers of rock on the village outskirts. She needed a new plan. And quickly:

gloomy thoughts were creeping back in, stalking her like a hungry leopard.

She sipped from her water bottle and sprinkled a few drops over her head and face, which was so hot the water almost sizzled. She mopped the sweat from the back of her neck and munched on a protein bar. *Pig! Where are you?* If only she had his supersonic snout, so she could sniff him out. He had to be here somewhere. If he wasn't, then where was he?

Just then, there was a loud squeal and grunt that rose well above all the other squeals and grunts – a squeal and grunt that she could understand, that was saying, *PEARLY! PEARLY! COME QUICK! I NEED HELP!*

CHAPTER 15

Pearly shot to her feet as a little pink pig with black bandit splotches across his eyes burst out of the jungle and galloped towards her.

I could smell you! Pig oinked as he took a flying leap into Pearly's arms. *I've been sniffing and sniffing and sniffing. And finally, there you were.*

Pearly's heart soared. Tears dribbled down her cheeks as she hugged Pig like she would never let him go.

"Where were you?" Pearly asked. "I've looked everywhere."

Exiled, Pig oinked. *The new king has put Ma in a pen outside the village. A pen!* Pig jumped free from Pearly's arms. *Come see!* he urged. *It's terrible.*

Pearly slung her adventure pack over one shoulder and raced after Pig who veered off the wide dirt path and down a winding track. The track took a few turns before it opened into a small clearing, where the air was thick with the smell of steaming pig muck, sticky mud and rotting vegetable scraps. There was a bamboo fence creating a pen and in the middle of the muddy patch lay a large pink pig with a black spotted behind. Pig's ma. The old sow was stretched out on her side, looking listless, folds of skin falling loosely from her belly, exposing her ribs.

Mamma mia! thought Pearly. Pig was right. *Questo è terribile!* This is terrible.

Ma, Pig oinked. *This is Pearly.*

Pig's ma didn't raise her head, or blink an eye, or acknowledge Pearly in any way.

She's so sick, Pig oinked. *At first, she didn't even know who I was. And then she couldn't understand me. It seems I talk Pig all wrong. But I've worked it out now.*

Pearly sat on a mossy log as Pig relayed what he had pieced together – a little from his mother, who had been too weak to say much, but mostly from some of his cousins. Apparently, as soon as King Alung Chu and his children disappeared, King Foom Chu had swiftly forbidden all pigs, chooks and people – except for some selected guards – from the compound and constructed the compound fence. He banished Pig's ma to the pen, declaring that she was not the Divine Sow and never had been. She was just a descendant and that she was old and hadn't produced a new sow and was useless to Ban Noa. That had made Ma and all the village heartsore. Life changed for the humans too.

King Foom Chu said things that made them troubled. They became terrified to venture into the jungle. And then the night rumbling and trembling began, which only made everyone more afraid. Ma had been healthy before that happened – old, but not frail and sick like she was now.

And, oinked Pig, *her illness has nothing to do with the Sacred Statue of the Divine Sow being displeased or the Balance being disturbed. It has everything to do with her food. I could smell it as soon as I found her. She is being poisoned, Pearly.*

Pearly was aghast. She stroked Pig's back and scratched behind his ears to try to calm him. "Smoky bacon to those worries, Pig," she whispered to him. "Remember Grandpa Woe always says, 'Knowledge is power'. It's in the *RAG*. It's how to survive sticky situations." She was saying this more for her benefit than for Pig's – she had to convince herself to be strong for Pig. "And we now have the knowledge to take action and help your ma." *If only she knew how.* But she didn't say that out loud.

Pearly looked about the pen for inspiration. Her eyes slid over the mouldy vegetable scraps and corn husks that littered the old sow's pen. They were stinky and not appetising at all, but the possibility that they were poisoned too made her stomach clench. Grandpa Woe was right not to trust King Foom Chu.

The man was despicable. But she would not let him get away with this. No one was going to harm Pig's ma. She stood up and pulled her machete out of its sleeve.

What are you doing? Pig squealed.

"I am using it to scoop away this food," she said. It was the only thing she could think to do. "I don't know what the poison is, so I don't want to touch it. But we have to get it away from your poor sick ma." Her boots squelched in the mud of the pen as she bent over and used the wide blade to scrape the food into a foul-smelling pile. She held her breath to avoid the stench and shoved the pile under the railings and out of the pen. Pig's ma gave a violent shudder. She still hadn't opened her eyes, and her breathing was slow and laboured. Pearly hoped they weren't too late. Again, she kept this to herself.

Pearly wiped the machete blade clean on a patch of grass and then slipped it back into its sleeve. "Now," she said to Pig, trying her best to sound confident and in control for Pig's sake, when in truth, she was far from it, "let's see if we can get some better food for her from your cousins. The non-poisoned kind. And get her well again."

Pearly, you are the best, Pig oinked. *I was so scared. I didn't know what to do.* He rubbed his ribs against her legs. *You are clever like your mum and dad and grandpa.*

Pearly didn't know about that, but it felt good to do something for Pig for once. To do something worthwhile.

Pig nudged his mother's side. *Hang on*, he pleaded. *We're going to make you well again. I promise.*

It was a promise Pearly hoped they could keep.

CHAPTER 16

Pig's ma was reluctant to eat the corn cobs and yams Pearly and Pig had gathered from the village pigs. But with some persistent encouragement from Pig, well, desperate snorting actually, she grunted, opened one eye and with little enthusiasm nibbled on a small piece of yam. It wasn't much, but it was a start.

Pearly made sure the food and some fresh water was within reach, then she persuaded Pig to leave his ma to rest and to help Pearly find Grandpa Woe and fill him in on what Pig had discovered. She knew he would be thrilled to see that Pig was safe and well.

The pair had just emerged from the jungle, when Pearly noticed someone poking about on the other side of the village. It was so unusual to see a person outside that it stopped Pearly in her tracks.

Whoever it was, they seemed to be looking for something, stepping into the jungle, pushing plants and vines aside, and then stepping out again. Why wasn't this person scared of the jungle like the rest of the village?

OINKY OINKY NO-NO! oinked Pig softly. *TROUBLE. I SMELL TROUBLE.*

Pearly and Pig crept across the village from hut to hut, until they reached the hut closest to the jungle edge. They slipped behind a rattan blind that hung over the back. Pearly pressed herself up against the blind and peeked out. The person was wearing an orange sarong and a sizeable rattan hat. It wasn't until a large fern frond was flicked out of the way that the person came into full view.

Pearly's breath caught in her throat. No way!

It was the king's son – Prince Tub Chu – the sneering one. He held his chin in one hand, tapping his cheek with a finger, as he stepped cautiously along the jungle edge. What was he looking for?

OINKY OINKY NO-NO! OINKY OINKY NO-NO! Pig whimpered over and over.

The prince was getting closer to where Pearly and Pig were hiding. They had to move before he spotted them.

Just then, the prince stopped. His sneering face broke into a gleeful smile. He picked up a slashed vine from the ground and then another.

Pearly held tight to Pig for strength as her knees began to knock together. Prince Tub had found the track Pearly's parents had cut into the jungle.

The prince turned his head from side to side. Pearly tensed as his eyes slid right past her and Pig. He tossed the slashed plants to the ground and disappeared into the jungle.

"He's following Mum and Dad," Pearly whispered to Pig. "I have a bad feeling about this."

OINKY OINKY NO-NO! Pig agreed.

Pearly didn't know what to do. Part of her felt that she should find Grandpa Woe and let him know. Another part of her felt that she should follow Tub and see what he was up to. *Knowledge is power.* If she followed him for a bit, she would have more to tell Grandpa Woe ... and her parents when they returned. This might be the lucky break they needed. She might find some key information. She might be useful, instead of a burden.

She looked back up to the village. She didn't know where to begin to look for Grandpa Woe, and her gut was telling her that she shouldn't wait until the sun dipped and they met to set up camp. That would be far too late. Pearly pushed away thoughts of what "too late" might mean. If she was ever going to be a super snoop and prove her worth, here was her chance.

Act quickly and decisively.

Number 6 in "Surviving Sticky Situations" in the *RAG.*

Her decision was made. "Come on, Pig," she said.

She slinked out from their hiding spot and tiptoed towards the jungle.

Pig took a couple of steps, then stopped. *Ma*, he oinked.

"We won't be long," breathed Pearly. "I promise. I just need to see what the prince is up to. We need information."

Pig snorted agreement and the two slipped onto the slender track that her parents had cut only a few hours before.

The jungle was ridiculously thick and noisy. Insects screamed. The undergrowth rattled with darting birds and lizards and who-knew-what. The ground was wet and mushy underfoot and the air dank. The path was so tight at times, it was difficult for Pearly to find where her parents had cut their track – it was as if the jungle was quickly reclaiming itself. Swallowing the path as soon as it was made. Pearly shuddered at the thought. This was no time to think about hungry jungles!

They had tramped for several minutes, doing their best to remain as quiet as possible. Pearly took each step with extreme caution, lest she crack a fallen stick or stumble on an exposed root. Pig picked his way slowly and steadily behind her.

Then, in the dense jungle ahead, Pearly spotted a glimpse of the prince's orange sarong – standing out like a tropical flower on a lush green canvas. Pearly held up her hand to stop. She crouched low and watched as Prince Tub shoved plants out of his way and trampled on others. He was certainly not treading lightly.

What was he looking for? Why was he following her parents?

The answer came almost immediately.

Prince Tub stopped abruptly. He laughed out loud. "*Bam hoon*!" he said in Anachakan. *Got you!* He took a couple of sideways steps to the left, then grabbed the trunk of a scrawny bent tree.

Blood rushed to Pearly's head. She couldn't believe what she was seeing.

Prince Tub wrapped his fingers around a strip of red material that was tied around the trunk, then he tugged it off and tucked it into the top of his sarong.

He was taking Ricky and Angel's track markers.

The track markers her parents used to ensure they could find their way back.

The ones to ensure Pearly and Grandpa Woe could find them if they didn't return.

CHAPTER 17

Pearly's mind swarmed with worries – worries humming and buzzing and thrumming right through her. A hive of worries! *Why would Prince Tub take her parents' markers? Did he* want *them to become lost? Were they in danger?* Then one large queen bee of a worry droned into Pearly's head. *Is this what happened to King Alung Chu and his children? Was Prince Tub somehow responsible?*

The thought was impossible to shift. And it seemed to make it impossible for Pearly to move. She had acted decisively and stepped boldly into the jungle like her parents and now look at her! Her newfound courage was pea-sized. She couldn't do this!

He's nearly out of sight, Pig oinked. *Quick.*

Pig started off down the track.

Pearly still couldn't move.

It was all too terrible. Italian phrases bubbled up inside her. Images of the danger her parents were in roiled like an angry sea through her mind.

GRICK! grunted Pig, which was Pig for, *Come on!* He doubled back and jabbed Pearly with his snout. *Hurry. Before we lose sight of him.*

Pearly still couldn't move.

Pearly! Pig pleaded. *Your parents need you. I smell trouble. Big trouble. We have to help. Smoky bacon and pork chops! Get moving.* He shoved her forcefully behind her knees. It was enough to jerk her forwards and snap her out of her trance.

"Smoky bacon," she muttered, in Pig, in Italian, in Anachakan, as her legs shakily carried her up the steep incline, following Pig. "Smoky bacon! Smoky bacon!"

Pig raced ahead. Pearly stumbled behind him until they reached the spot where Prince Tub had stolen her parents' red marker.

"Wait," Pearly whispered.

She slid her pack from her back, rummaged inside, and pulled out a stripy neck scarf. It wasn't as long as her parents' markers, but it was long enough to tie around one of the thinner branches.

Good thinking! Pig oinked. *See – you're clever. You can do this.*

"No point us getting lost – or swallowed too!" added Pearly grimly.

They veered left as the prince had done and traipsed to the top of the incline then down into another valley, where at the bottom, Pearly spied a flicker of that orange sarong, a flash of the large rattan hat. She ducked behind a tree fern with Pig and watched.

Prince Tub had stopped again and dread quickly found a home in Pearly's stomach. To the prince's left was another red band around a swirl of vines. He untied it, tucked it into his sarong, and then he was off again.

Pearly and Pig allowed the prince to disappear, before heading off and replacing the red marker, this time with a length of rope.

They shot off to the left, the track getting slimmer, the canopy thicker – the heavy roof of green stealing away the sun. It was becoming so dark that Pearly was having difficulty seeing the track or any sight of Prince Tub either, which only made the hairs on the back of her neck stick up. *Where was he?* A shiver raced down her spine.

Pearly slowed down, eyes wide, ears straining. Still there was no sign of the prince, or any red markers for that matter.

Pig put his snout to the ground, waving it back and forth. *I can still smell him*, he oinked. *But it is getting faint. I can also smell mud and hear water.*

It was at this moment that Pearly heard it too – the unmistakeable sound of rushing water. A creek? Or waterfall perhaps? Somewhere close. She ducked under a fallen tree, then over the crawling roots of a fig, pushing wet leaves and vines out of her way. Freshly slashed branches littered the ground, and she felt reassured that they were still on the track her parents had cut. She kept her eyes peeled for the red markers and, of course, Prince Tub's orange sarong.

The track dipped and then turned slightly.

Then stopped.

Pearly yelped with shock.

The toes of her boots were hanging over the edge of a muddy cliff that plunged to a fast-flowing creek below, the brown waters sliding over boulders and crashing against mossy logs.

Pig screeched to a halt beside her, then put his nose to the ground and sniffed to his left then right.

This way, he oinked and trotted off to the right where a path barely wider than Pearly's boots slithered between the cliff edge and the jungle.

Pearly took each step with extreme care, her heart thudding, her legs trembling. Misty spray filled the air and now that they were out from beneath the jungle canopy, Pearly noted that the sun had already dipped behind the distant peaks to the west. Long shadows stretched out before her. It was getting late. Soon it would be dark.

Once again, she was torn. Should she keep going and risk being stuck in the jungle all night? Or should she go back now while she could still see and alert Grandpa Woe about Prince Tub following her parents?

The decision was made for her, because at that precise moment of indecision, her boot caught on a raised tree root and she fell head over heels. She flung out her hand to save herself, but her hand only found the edge of the muddy cliff. Momentum and her heavy adventure pack did the rest, and she was sent tumbling over the cliff to the waters below.

CHAPTER 18

Pearly slid and tumbled and slid some more until she landed with a painful thud, face first in the muddy bank beside the creek. Her head was spinning and every bone in her body seemed to ache. She lay still for a moment, catching her breath, then she wiggled her fingers followed by her toes inside her boots. Nothing broken – she hoped. Cautiously, she turned herself over onto her back, spitting out the globs of mud that filled her mouth.

Pearly! Pearly!

Pearly sat up and gingerly looked up to see a distressed Pig perched at the edge of the cliff, peering down at her.

Pearly! Are you all right? he oinked.

Pearly wasn't sure how to answer. She was alive, she knew that, but she felt woozy and shaken. Her ribs ached and so did her left knee and thigh. She slid her eyes over the muddy trail her tumble had forged down the cliff face and was grateful that the cliff was mostly mud and grasses, rather than rocks and boulders.

"I'm okay ... I think," she called up to Pig, her voice mud-raspy and scare-shaky. She leant on her right hand and tried to stand but couldn't quite manage it. Her ankle throbbed painfully.

Wait! called Pig. *I'm coming.*

Pearly tilted her head to see what he was doing, but he was nowhere to be seen. The sound of galloping trotters pierced the air and the next thing, Pig was flying off the cliff edge. He soared through the air – who said pigs can't fly – and landed with a splash and a squelch onto a muddy ledge about halfway down the cliff.

Hold tight. Nearly there, her little hero oinked. Pig slid off the ledge and picked a slippery path down the rest of the cliff to the bank. He charged up to where Pearly sat.

Anything broken? Can you walk? Pig oinked frantically. *Oh Pearly, you had me worried. Smoky bacon, I thought you were ...* Pig didn't finish, and he didn't need to. They both knew what he thought.

"I'm okay. I'm sore and a little dizzy, but I don't think I've broken anything, though my ankle is throbbing. But what are we going to do now? How will we get back up? It's going to be night soon."

The two adventurers surveyed their surroundings. The cliff loomed behind them, and it seemed unlikely either of them would be able to climb back up. In front of them was a narrow bank of sticky mud that framed a waterhole, where the gushing creek pooled, before spilling water thick with silt over large boulders to then rush downstream. On the opposite bank was a grassy clearing in front of another steep jungle-filled hill.

"*Mamma mia*!" Pearly thumped the ground with her fist. "I'm so clumsy!" *Goffa*. (Italian) *Tollpatsch*. (German.) *Orr-arr-orr*. (Macaque.) *Gruntity-huff*. (Pig.) "Now we won't be able to follow the prince and replace the markers and warn Mum and Dad. And Grandpa Woe will be at the hut and wondering where the heck I am. Oh, Pig, Dad was right – I shouldn't be here." So much for her quest to find information. She had failed again.

Stop that silly talk, oinked Pig. *You tripped. That's all. And you were trying to save your parents. So don't be so hard on yourself.*

Pearly used both hands to push herself up to stand. She was still a little dizzy. She took a couple of shaky steps in a circle, avoiding putting weight on her left ankle, trying to work out what to do.

"But ..."

Buts don't help. Coming up with a plan will. Pig squelched across the muddy bank and plunged into the waterhole.

"What are you doing?" yelled Pearly, her eyebrows drawn together.

Pig's little legs kicked frantically, his snout poking up to the sky. *Checking out the other side, of course!*

Pearly watched as Pig piggy-paddled across the waterhole and then stepped onto the grassy shore. He gave himself a fierce shake and immediately started sniffing around.

"Can you smell Mum and Dad?" Pearly asked.

No. No humans, except you. Lots of animals though. I think this might be a watering hole for ... Pig stopped.

"For what?"

Ah, Asian elephants ... sniff sniff *... clouded leopards ...* sniff, sniff, sniff *... tigers and, ah, gibbons, lots of types ...* sniff *... oh – giant flying squirrels and very scary wild pigs – so many scents!*

Pearly gulped. She knew enough about animal behaviour to know that most animals came to watering holes in the evening and early morning – or during the night. This was not good news. You didn't have to be a rocket scientist to realise that there was little chance of getting back to Ban Noa or even back up to her parents' track today. They had to find somewhere to camp – and it probably shouldn't be on the edge of a popular waterhole for leopards, tigers and wild elephants, to name but a few.

She retrieved her adventure pack that was stuck in the mud several metres away from where she landed and swiped mud from it. It looked a little squished, and she hoped nothing was broken, but was relieved to see her machete still secure in its pouch.

If they were ever going to make it out of here, she was going to need all the machete skills she could muster.

But machete skills were not all she needed. She needed her father's compass and maps, a solid plan and most of all some Woe courage. And she didn't have any of them.

CHAPTER 19

They set up camp slightly upstream from the waterhole. Here, the creek hurried through a narrow channel near the northern bank. A large muddy quagmire stretched between the southern bank and the cliff above, and a rocky overhang provided a small shelter and enough dry flat ground for Pearly and Pig to sleep on.

Pig had surveyed the scents and had come to the conclusion that only a few animals approached the waterhole from this side of the bank near the wide bog, so it was reasonably safe.

Pearly wasn't too keen on the word "reasonably" but she agreed that this was probably their best option. She didn't like the thought of "probably" either.

It was dark now and a light rain was falling, and Pearly was grateful for the shelter the overhang provided. They were in the foothills of the craggy highlands, and the night-time air was cool. Pearly pulled on her weatherproof jacket and strapped on

Pig's rain jacket. She squished a mosquito on her hand.

One of the first lessons Pearly was taught when she started her Adventurologist training was making sure her adventure pack was well stocked with lightweight essentials. And, boy, was Pearly grateful for that right now. But she needed to be careful because she only had enough food left for herself for three days max and one day for Pig, as the family had divided Pig's supplies between them. She wondered if Pig would be keen on her Madras curry chicken if the need arose. She hoped she wouldn't need to find out.

Pig sat below the lip of the overhang, as if standing guard, as Pearly busied herself with boiling water on her camp burner and opening the meal sachets. She had got the water from the creek – to save her own supplies – and was relieved to find that it tasted sweet and fresh, with only a hint of mud.

By the time their meal was finished, the rain had become heavier, and they crawled further under the ledge. Pearly threw her tarp over the top of them and snuggled close to Pig.

She closed her eyes and tried not to think about the mess they were in. But questions stubbornly circled through her mind. What would Grandpa Woe think when she didn't turn up at their meeting spot? What was Prince Tub up to? Were her parents in danger? Worst of all was the feeling that she was trapped in this gully, on this creek edge. Even if they could find a way back up, she was certain they would be horribly lost.

She muttered *smoky bacon* over and over to try to stop the thoughts and to trick herself into sleep. She said it in Italian and German and Pig and Anachakan and Icelandic and Macaque Monkey and in all of the twenty-seven languages she was fluent in. It didn't seem to help.

Water gushed and splashed through the creek channel. Rain pounded the muddy mire. It dripped from the overhang. Branches creaked. Night birds called. Leaves and sticks cracked as animals thrashed their way through the undergrowth. A distant growl shuddered through the deep gully.

It was going to be a long night.

A loud trumpeting abruptly woke Pearly before the sun had barely peeked above the horizon. Pearly flicked off the tarpaulin and sat bolt upright.

Pig squealed, OINKY OINKY NO-NO! OINKY OINKY NO-NO! *Trouble. I smell trouble. And ... elephants!*

And there they were. In the hazy pre-dawn mist, not one, but two elephants – a mother and her calf – screaming their distress, the calf thigh-deep in the muddy bog.

WARRR! WARRR! WAAAAARRRRRRRRR! *HELP!*
HELP! HEEEELLLLLPPPPP!

Pearly raced towards the pair.

The mother held her trunk in the air, her ears wide open and screamed a warning, ROWARRR! ROWARRR! ROWARRRRRR! *STAY AWAY!*

She flapped her ears and stamped her foot in the mud, spraying orange globs everywhere. ROWARRR! ROWARRR! ROWARRRRRR! she repeated, *STAY AWAY!* She stepped closer to her calf and curled her trunk protectively over the youngster's back.

Pearly and Pig stood at the edge of the bog, as the calf squealed and whimpered and tried desperately to step out of the thick orange mire, while the mother pushed the calf's behind with her foot and shoved its side with her trunk, their cries of distress growing louder and more panicked.

We have to help, oinked Pig.

"I know," agreed Pearly. "But how?"

Can you talk to the mother, calm her down? suggested Pig.

"I guess I can try." Pearly had been intrigued with elephants and the way they communicated since she went on a holiday with Esmeralda to Malaysia when she was about seven. Her grandmother had helped to fund an elephant rescue sanctuary on the east coast and Pearly was able to spend a glorious week at the sanctuary helping to look after three calves and one adult female that had recently been rescued from an elephant tourist park where they had been mistreated. She had since returned to the sanctuary twice more and loved having long chats with the young calves. Apart from Pig, Elephant was her favourite animal language.

Pearly took off her waterproof jacket and tossed it out of the way. She took a tentative step towards the elephants. The mother immediately bristled, flapped her ears and trumpeted her anger at Pearly, a long, loud torrent of warning and distress and fury that shook the trees. Pearly knew she meant business. The mother would do anything to protect her calf. Pearly stopped and waited for her to quieten. Then she dipped her head and held one arm out in front of her, her palm open. RARARAH, RARARAH, she said, her voice croaky. *Can I help?* RARARAH, RARARAH, she repeated, louder and more confidently this time.

The calf squealed and tried to scramble out of the bog, and Pearly worried that she had used the wrong sounds. But the mother dipped her head and cocked her ear to one side, flinging her trunk from side to side, her aggression diminished somewhat. Pearly hoped she was reading the situation correctly.

Please, let me help, she tried.

The calf kicked its front legs up, and almost made

it over the lip of the bog, only to slip and then sink back deeper.

The mother hooked her trunk under its belly, as she made soothing noises to calm it, but the mud was too thick.

Pearly took slow cautious steps down the bank towards the elephants, echoing the mother's soothing sounds, fingers crossed that she wasn't going to upset the mother more.

It seemed to be working. The mother wasn't responding to Pearly's pleas, but she wasn't getting agitated about them either. If anything, she was confused.

The overnight rain had created muddy pools all the way across the bank. Pearly picked her way around them, looking for the least boggy route. All the while, she kept BR-BR-BR-ing, echoing the mother's noises, which sounded like a cross between an outboard motor and a long rumbly fart.

At last, she was close to the lip of the bog the little calf was stuck in. Its ears were limp, the hairs on its back slicked down with the goo. The mother loomed large on the other side of the hole. She flung her trunk in the air and trumpeted WARRR! *HELP!*

Pearly took it as a request. *I will*, she replied. The mother shook her head, looking baffled.

Pearly squelched through the mud towards the back

of the calf. Now that she was here, how was she going to help? She remembered watching some videos with Esmeralda about elephant rescues – and they involved much pushing and shoving and heavy earthmoving equipment. One video even had a helicopter join in the effort. Was she kidding herself?

The calf whimpered and the mother wailed. And Pearly knew she had to try.

She knelt directly behind the little calf. She patted its rump calmly and talked to it, so she wouldn't alarm it further, like the way the mahouts had taught her at the sanctuary. The mother seemed to sense what Pearly was doing. She positioned herself in front of the calf and hooked her trunk around the calf's trunk.

Pearly took the cue and leaned her weight against the calf's behind and pushed with all her might, groaning with the strain of it, as the mother tried to pull the calf with her trunk. Pearly slipped and fell – splat – into the mud, but she pushed herself up and leaned back in, *Come on, little one*, she crooned. *You can do it.*

Pearly pushed. The mother pulled. The calf kicked its legs and tried to scramble out. Pearly fell splat into the mud again. Nothing worked. Pearly was now a mud monster, covered from head to toe with the gooey sludge. She wiped her eyes and mouth. She had to come up with a different plan. If only she had a spare digger, she thought ridiculously. But that gave her an idea. She didn't have a digger or backhoe or anything mechanical, but she did have hands, and she had Pig who was a champion digger.

Pig, she called. *Let's get that jacket off you! We're going to have to dig her out!*

CHAPTER 20

Hot morning sunlight streamed through the thick waves of humidity rising off the water and mingling with the already steamy air. Pearly's head thumped. Her back burned. Her ribs were tender and her injured ankle throbbed, the swelling rubbing against her boot, but she couldn't give up.

The little calf was panicking now – especially when it sighted Mud Monster Pearly and Pig who was, well, a pig, and not necessarily a friend to a little calf. The wild pigs along the Mekong had a reputation for being fierce.

The mother elephant was becoming increasingly frantic, but she obeyed Pearly's request that they swap positions, so Pearly could try to dig a channel out of the boggy hole.

Pearly leant into the hole and scraped back lumps of mud to form a path out, scooping out as much as she could with her hands and arms. Much fell immediately back in, but eventually a U-shaped channel started to emerge. Pig worked behind and alongside Pearly, using his snout to push the mud out of the way and to make the channel wider and deeper. It reminded Pearly of their younger days of digging tunnels and ditches on the banks of the Lemon Tree River below Woe Mansion. They could do this.

The channel widened and the little calf tried desperately to clamber out, only to slip back down. The mother used her large foot to push her calf from behind. When that didn't work, she used the long length of her trunk and finally her hip and sides to push and push, until finally the calf scrambled out of the hole on unsteady legs. It wobbled across the muddy bank to solid ground. The mother followed, circling it and prodding it with her trunk, crooning a soft rumbly BREEP, BREEP, BREEP, reassuring the calf it was okay now.

The mother turned and flapped her ears at Pearly and Pig.

Thank you! she trumpeted. *Hurray!* It was such a happy trumpet.

Pearly pushed her muddy self out of the bog and followed Pig back to their camp. The elephants lingered beside her. Pearly pulled her last banana from her adventure pack and offered it to the calf. The calf gobbled it down. Pearly washed her face and hands with water from a bowl she had left out overnight, and then pulled out a protein bar for breakfast. Pig turned his nose up at the bar and resorted to grazing nearby on grass and digging around for some roots and berries, as he loudly lamented the days of Angel's pizzas and corn fritters. The calf scratched the mud off its back on the sides of the cliff that led up to the track Pearly had fallen down only the day before.

The mother sidled up to Pearly and tapped her on her shoulder with her trunk. Pearly peered deep into her gentle eyes, framed with long coarse eyelashes and circles of wrinkles. She seemed calm finally, so Pearly introduced herself and tried to strike up a conversation.

She could tell that the elephant was unsure about talking to a human, but she was also grateful to Pearly for helping to rescue her calf, and she relayed that to Pearly with great passion. The mother was known as Samam. The calf was a daughter and her name was Bim. She was a mischievous daughter, who often got herself into trouble. And to confirm this, Bim trumpeted gleefully and cavorted up and down the narrow strip of grass, scarily close to the bog.

Bim! called Samam. Bim looked up, but then spied Pig trotting close by and took off after him, tail swooshing.

Pearly laughed at Bim's antics, and she wondered if her parents sometimes felt the same way about Pearly. This thought made her stomach drop, as she was suddenly reminded of the mess she was in – and the danger her own family might be facing. And the fact she had failed at the one thing her mother had asked her to do – find information.

Samam sensed her change in mood.

What is wrong, little Pearly? she asked.

What's wrong? So many things! Pearly clenched her teeth and fought back tears.

I'm lost, Pearly said finally. Which was the truth, but only part of it. She was lost, but she also didn't know what she should do. Should she try to find her parents and warn them, or should she try to find Ban Noa and tell Grandpa about Prince Tub? She didn't know how to convey all that to Samam, so she changed the subject. *Bim seems to like Pig*, she said.

Samam and Pearly watched Bim as she tried to entice Pig to play a game of chasey. Pig was teasing her, pretending to chase and then stop. Pearly found herself laughing despite her anguish. Bim stopped and gazed at the giggling Pearly, her ears framing her face like two sides of a love heart. She was adorable, that was for sure.

As Pearly returned Bim's gaze, something caught her eye. Movement. On the opposite side of the creek. Branches and vines swayed, leaves crackled. A large colourful bird took flight. Pearly squinted into the distance as a pale brown monkey swung out from a vine, soared across the creek and bog to land right beside Bim, who scampered off in alarm.

"Wah-Wah!" Pearly raced to greet the little monkey.

Wah-Wah jumped into her arms, then climbed onto her shoulder, then head, then back to the ground, all the while chittering and chattering and squealing with delight.

Found you, banana head! At last! Wah-Wah said. *Your old human is very worried. He thinks the jungle gobbled you up.*

Pearly crouched beside Wah-Wah. Pig joined them.

You found the pig. That is good. Wah-Wah jumped on Pig's back. Pig bucked him off. *You have bananas?*

Pearly shook her head. The jungle was full of wild banana trees. Why couldn't he find his own?

No bananas for you, cheeky! Pearly replied. *Have you seen my parents? The other old humans?*

No. No humans in jungle.

Pearly held her head with both hands, her parents' predicament crashing in on her again.

Pig put his snout in the air and sniffed deeply. *Still no scent*, he oinked.

Wah-Wah was now curled in Samam's trunk. It seemed like they knew each other.

I have to find my parents, Wah-Wah, she told the monkey. *Can you help me get back up onto the track up there?*

Humans not there. Wah-Wah jumped down from Samam and ambled over to Pearly.

I know they're not there, Pearly explained, *but they went that way.*

No! No humans. Only you. Wah-Wah stood face to face with Pearly, his banana breath fouling the air.

What do you mean?

I asked. And jungle said only you.

Pearly was confused. And so was Pig. He grunted and huddled close to Pearly.

Pearly shrugged and shook her head to show Wah-Wah that she didn't understand.

I asked the jungle line. Wah-Wah jumped up and down with excitement that Pearly couldn't comprehend. *We animals look out for each other. We talk. I sent the message out, and it came back with one. One young human near drinking hole. How do you think I found you, banana head?*

Pearly's heart sank. "*Mamma mia. Questo è terribile!*" *This is terrible.* If her parents weren't in the jungle, then where were they? Had the jungle really swallowed them?

Samam must have sensed Pearly's distress, as she leant her trunk on Pearly's shoulder, crooning softly as she had done with Bim. *Breep, breep, breep.*

It was indeed a calming noise, but Pearly was past being calmed.

"Pig! We have to go back to Ban Noa," Pearly said – she could see no other way.

Thank goodness! oinked Pig. *I need to see Ma.*

Pearly's face flared with shame. She had forgotten all about Pig's ma. Poor Pig, he must have been beside himself with worry all night, and he never said a word.

Samam tapped her trunk on Pearly's shoulder again. *What is troubling you?* she breeped gently.

We need to get back to Ban Noa – the humans' village. And we don't know how.

I will take you there, Samam replied.

Pearly couldn't believe her ears. *You will?*

Of course. You helped me, now I will help you. Come on! Saman stamped her front foot, swished her tail and called to Bim.

Good! Good! The little monkey did a happy jig and then clambered up through some hanging vines. *See you there! Bring bananas.* And he was gone.

Pearly swiftly gathered up her things into her adventure pack. She retrieved the muddy rain jackets and shoved them, mud and all, inside the pack, and pulled on her hat.

"Quick!" she said to Pig. "Samam is going to show us the way back to Ban Noa."

Just then, the large elephant lowered herself onto her wrinkly backside and then worked her front legs out in front of her. *Get on*, she breeped.

Pearly was aghast. She couldn't ride an elephant. Both Esmeralda and Grandpa Woe would have a fit. It was one of the few things her grandparents agreed upon. They were absolutely united in their views about the exploitation of animals. *I can't*, said Pearly. *It's wrong.*

You can. I am inviting you. And the pig. This will be the quickest way. Sit near my head. That is best.

It felt all kinds of wrong, but Pearly knew she couldn't refuse. She awkwardly climbed up onto Samam's back and straddled her legs over her neck. It took her a moment or two to get her balance, then she called to Pig.

You're not serious, are you? Pig oinked.

"'Fraid so," Pearly replied. "Come on up! Your ma awaits."

AROO! AROO! AROO! Pig muttered, before taking a running jump and clambering onto Samam's bent knee, and then up her side. Pearly reached down and helped him over Samam's shoulder.

Put Pig in front of you, then put your hands on my head to keep balance, Samam instructed.

Pig stretched himself sideways across Samam's neck, legs jutting out on either side. *I don't like this*, he squealed. AROO! AROO! AROO!

Samam called to Bim to join her, then to Pearly, *Brah-arah. Hold tight.*

126

The elephant eased herself up. Pearly swayed. She bent right over Pig to keep her balance. She pressed her palms on Samam's head, and pushed herself back up, as the elephant trundled off, along the bank to the waterhole. She waded across the silty water, finding a shallow path for Bim to follow.

Pearly held on for dear life.

CHAPTER 21

Samam took great care as she plodded along beside the creek. At times she waded right through the middle of the murky water.

It was a long way down to the ground from Samam's back and that made it one scary ride for Pearly. Pearly swayed and rocked and bumped and, at times, almost slid right off. Pig kept his body rigid, muttering AROO! AROO! AROO! He was not enjoying the ride.

Finally, Samam, with Bim trotting merrily behind her, left the creek and lumbered up a sloping bank and into the scrub. She found an open grassy patch and lowered herself to the ground.

Pig was off in a shot. Pearly flicked her legs to one side and slid down Samam's back, landing painfully on her injured ankle.

The village is that way. Samam pointed with her trunk. *We can't come closer. But you will find it. Look for the rocks pointing to the sky.*

Pearly hugged Samam and rubbed the top of her head, before Samam swayed up to her feet. Little Bim moseyed around the clearing, pulling up grass and sniffing the bordering plants.

Thank you so much, Pearly breeped.

BARR-WARRRRAHHH! Samam trumpeted happily.

Pearly was reluctant to leave. She had grown fond of this elephant and her calf. But Pig was eager, and he galloped up to Pearly and nudged her legs with his snout.

Come on, Pearly, he oinked. *I need to see Ma.*

Pearly thanked Samam again, gave her and Bim another hug, patting their rough hides one last time. She adjusted the shoulder straps of her pack, caked off some dry mud from her trousers and shirt and headed off in the direction Samam had indicated.

It was then, after the adrenaline-filled elephant rescue and ride was behind her, that Pearly realised how stiff and sore she was. And not just her ankle, which was making her hobble, her left thigh and knee, her ribs and her neck all ached. No doubt she was covered in bruises.

The jungle was thin and scrubby for only a short distance and Pearly had to use her machete to cut a way through. But true to Samam's word, soon the towering moss-covered fingers of rock pointing to the sky came into view.

Relief filled Pearly. She couldn't wait to find Grandpa Woe and tell him what she had witnessed and what the jungle line had said about her parents. He would know what to do.

The grunts and squeals of many pigs rose above the insect buzz and bird calls, and with a few more slashes of her machete, they were at Ban Noa, right beside one of the rocky towers. Pearly and Pig stopped behind it, taking cover behind the snaking creepers that tangled out to one side. Pearly leaned out and surveyed the village.

Pearly grimaced. There was something still not right about this village. Pig snorted and grunted and oinked, OINKY OINKY NO-NO! OINKY OINKY NO-NO! He obviously felt the same way.

But there was something other than the eerie air that cloaked the village contributing to Pearly's unease. The whole time the Woes had been in Ban Noa the villagers seemed to disappear – except for that time when they were summoned to the king's compound. Ban Noa had the feel of a deserted ghost village, home only to pigs and squawking chickens. The pigs still lay about in shady patches or cantered around in the dust, chickens pecked at the ground or roosted under the huts, but right now there were also people about. A woman stirred a pot under her hut, another washed some yams. Children sat on ramps or wandered about with the pigs. Two men leaned up against a hut talking softly. Another attended to a broken shutter.

It was not exactly the carefree hive of activity that Grandpa Woe had described – the people in her line of vision were quiet and watchful. But at least they were out of their huts and going about their business. Pearly wondered what had changed. Perhaps Grandpa Woe had been able to find some friends and had showed them that they had nothing to fear from them.

She nodded at Pig and the two slipped out from behind the pillar.

Immediately, the children were called inside. The cooking pot pulled off the fire. The broken shutter left hanging. Everyone disappeared inside. It was as if they were villains – wild and dangerous. Pearly's pulse thudded in her ears.

She limped along the dirt path between huts, her eyes flitting from side to side. She needed to find Grandpa Woe – and fast.

Pig had his nose to the ground, sniffing. *I can smell Ma*, he squealed, his squeal laced with relief.

"What about Grandpa Woe?" Pearly whispered. "Can you smell where he is?"

Pig sniffed long and deep, and then longer and deeper. He moved to the other side of the pathway and sniffed some more. He slipped under a hut to the next pathway, sniffing constantly.

He was taking his time. "Pig?" she called, her eyebrows drawn together. "Pig?"

Pig scampered back. Pearly could tell by the look on his little pink face that the news was not good. *Sorry, Pearly*, he oinked. *I can't smell Grandpa Woe anywhere. Not even a leftover trace.*

This was not what Pearly wanted to hear.

CHAPTER 22

Pig was desperate to see his ma, but he was also insistent that they find Grandpa Woe first. His ma's scent was strong, he told Pearly, and he sensed she was doing okay. But the absence of Grandpa Woe's scent was making him twitchy.

First, they headed for the spot where Pearly was meant to meet with Grandpa Woe and set up camp. Pearly scanned the area carefully. There was nothing there to indicate that he had even been there, let alone stayed the night, and Pig still couldn't detect even the tiniest skerrick of scent.

It rained last night, Pig offered. *Any scent would be washed away. Maybe he stayed in a hut?*

Pearly had had those thoughts too. But she also knew that Grandpa Woe would have been worried about her. Maybe he had gone looking for her. But then she remembered Wah-Wah saying that he had seen Grandpa Woe – when and where was that?

And of course, the jungle line and Pig's snout had both said there were no other humans in the jungle.

They wandered all through the village. Pearly tried desperately to push away the dreadful thought that the jungle had somehow swallowed him too. Finally, in desperation, she decided she needed to ask someone. They might be afraid of her, but she had no reason to be afraid of them, did she?

On shaky legs and with Pig right beside her, she staggered up a ramp to the closest hut. She knocked on the bamboo door. The door swung open, releasing aromas of coconut and rice. Inside, a family sat on a mat, eating from bowls. They gasped at the sight of her.

"Sorry," Pearly said in Anachakan. "I am looking for my grandpa. You might know him. Gordon Woe. He is old and was wearing an orange hat and a faded button-down shirt and khaki shorts and ..." She was babbling and close to tears. The family peered at her, bewildered. "Please. I need to find him."

"Out." A woman who looked to be the mother stood and shooed Pearly away with her hand. "You must not be here. Out."

Pearly backed away. "But I need ..."

"Out!" An elderly man stood and joined the woman.

Pearly and Pig turned and scurried down the ramp and away.

Let's see Ma, Pig suggested.

Pearly squatted beside Pig and scratched between his ears. "Of course," she said. "That's an excellent plan." She chewed on her bottom lip as she surveyed the stilted huts around her. Where was Grandpa Woe?

Pearly struggled to her feet and then hobbled along the track behind Pig. The straps of her adventure pack dug into her shoulders and it was starting to feel as if it were filled with rocks.

With some relief, she collapsed onto a grassy patch as soon as they reached the sow's exile pen. She was doubly relieved when she saw that Pig's ma was lying on her stomach, her snout resting on her trotters – it seemed the new food must have helped her regain some strength. The sow lifted her head and oinked with happiness as Pig galloped towards her.

Ma! Pig oinked back. He skidded under the rail and smothered his mother in licks and nudges and piggy cuddles.

Pearly leant back on her arms and watched the happy reunion. Pig and his ma grunted and oinked and squealed in a piggy language that Pearly could barely understand. She was only able to pick up the odd word or two, but the tone of it radiated sheer joy.

Joy. That was something she needed. And rest. Time to collect her thoughts. She felt so alone. It was up to Pig and her now – just like in Antarctica. And like in Antarctica she cast her mind to the *RAG* for help.

They were definitely in a sticky situation, so she tried to visualise the chapter about surviving sticky situations.

Number 7 loomed large in her mind: *don't panic*. That was easier said than done, and she could already feel a growing ball of panic pushing against her chest. But it was Numbers 1 and 2 that offered her the most inspiration: *take initiative* and *think outside the square*. This was definitely a situation that called for both of these. She needed to be creative in order to come up with a new plan, which was one of the basics of Adventurologing: *planning is everything*. But also, *be prepared to be spontaneous, when plans don't go to plan*. Well, nothing had gone to plan so far! So all she could do was to come up with a better plan.

Simple!

As if.

The squeaks and squeals went up a notch and pulled Pearly out of her thoughts. It was lovely to watch Pig and his ma. But it also made her long for her own family even more. Where were they? What had happened to them?

King Foom Chu's warning rang through her head: *The Balance has been disturbed, the Sacred Statue of the Divine Sow is displeased, and the jungle is swallowing all who venture too far from Ban Noa.*

Had the jungle swallowed Grandpa Woe and her mum and dad? A shiver shunted right through her.

Don't panic, she reminded herself. After all, she had ventured into the jungle, but it hadn't swallowed her. A stabbing twinge in her ribs made her wonder if she had just been lucky. She could have been seriously hurt from the fall.

Pig ducked out of the pen and jogged over to Pearly, his tongue hanging out, panting. He plopped down in the shade beside her.

Ma is feeling so much better, he oinked. *But we need to get her more food. One of Foom's guards brought her a bucketful this morning – and it stinks of that poison. Ma hasn't touched it. She has lots of information for us.*

Pig told Pearly that his ma had seen Grandpa Woe late yesterday, just before dark. She recognised him from his previous stays. He looked jittery. Pig had also found out some more about what was going on in the village. Like Pig's cousins, his ma blamed everything on King Foom Chu. She thought something was going on in the compound – and also *behind* the compound. It was forbidden grounds – for the villagers and the pigs.

She says that we need to explore the jungle behind the compound, Pig oinked. *But we must not get caught. Or ...*

"Or what?" Pearly asked.

She wouldn't say.

Pearly tried to ignore the sinking feeling in her stomach and be glad that they finally had a new lead.

"I wonder if Grandpa Woe went there too?" Pearly said.

Grandpa Woe wasn't in the village. And he wasn't in the jungle. Pig couldn't detect his scent near the compound. They really had no choice but to check out behind the compound. They were seriously running out of options.

"Let's get some food and water for your ma, and then I guess we need to see what lies behind King Foom's compound."

It wasn't much of a plan, but at least it *was* a plan.

CHAPTER 23

Pearly and Pig agreed that they should wait until it was dark before searching behind the compound. A night-time search was a terrifying thought, but so was being caught by one of Foom Chu's guards – and there was more chance of that in the daylight. So after they had finished removing Ma's poisoned food and replacing it with fresh corn cobs and yams that Pig's cousins had shared from their feed troughs, they decided to take a hike across the rickety bamboo bridge over the muddy trickle of a creek, and down to the old Ban Noa, just in case Grandpa Woe had gone there for some reason.

It was a long trek and, not surprisingly, the macaques weren't too thrilled to see the girl and pig again. They screeched and wailed and barked their disapproval, which was enough for Pearly and Pig to turn swiftly and head back out. Grandpa Woe wasn't there, and Pig's snout knew it even before they had entered the village.

On their way out, they spotted Wah-Wah sitting on a pile of bananas under one of the abandoned huts. Pearly laughed at Wah-Wah's banana obsession. Then she was struck by a puzzling thought. Why was there a great pile of bananas here? She crouched low and noticed that enormous piles of bananas were scattered throughout the village.

Wah-Wah jumped up and down on the spot when he saw Pearly. He shoved a banana into his mouth then chittered, *Banana head back! Samam save you!*

Wah-Wah vaulted onto Pig's back and then leapt onto Pearly's shoulder. Pearly scratched under his chin. *When did you see my grandpa?* she chittered, as she scratched. *The oldest human?*

Wah-Wah's mouth turned down and he put a finger to his mouth, looking thoughtful. *Don't remember*, he said, and scurried off to get another banana.

Pearly followed. *I need your help, Wah-Wah. Was it day or night?*

The little monkey shoved another banana into his mouth and chewed slowly before replying. *Last light*, he said. *Before dark. He look very bad. That why Wah-Wah went looking for you.*

Pearly hated to hear this. She shouldn't have gone off without telling him. A warm rush of blood crept up her neck and across her face. *Have you seen him today?* Pearly asked.

Wah-Wah stuck the tip of one finger in his mouth and shook his head. *No!* Then he demolished another banana.

This monkey has a banana problem, oinked Pig.

Pearly nodded her agreement. *Where do all these bananas come from?* she asked.

Wah-Wah turned his head from side to side. He crept closer to Pearly, using Pig to shield his view from the other monkeys. *The jungle provides*, he whispered. And then he shot off, up a tree, swinging from branch to branch until he was out of sight.

That was very strange, oinked Pig.

"Exceptionally," agreed Pearly. "We better get going or it will be dark before we reach the new Ban Noa."

Night had indeed fallen by the time Pearly and Pig had made it back to Ban Noa, and the eerie atmosphere of the daytime village seemed amplified. A few families had ventured out of their huts to gather briefly around cooking fires. Many huts glowed with torchlight. Pigs and hens lay sleeping in huddles underneath the huts. It was all too quiet. It made Pearly jittery.

Pearly and Pig left the village to see Ma, who was really starting to look much better; there was some life in her eyes now.

Pig happily chatted and snuggled with his ma, but Pearly was soon restless. Her parents had been gone for two days now and Grandpa vanished for at least a day, and it was proving difficult for Pearly not to imagine the worst. She couldn't let her mind go there. She needed to get going before she chickened out.

She put her hat in her pack, made sure everything was secure inside and then called out to Pig. It was time.

Pig said goodbye to his ma and followed Pearly as she trudged back to the village. Once they reached the clearing, they stayed close to the jungle border, dashing from rock pillar to rock pillar, trying to stay out of view as much as possible. It was a brilliant night. The stars were bright and a half-moon rested above the treetops. Normally, Pearly loved nights like this. But tonight she had hoped to melt into the night, to be one with the shadows, but it was far too bright for that.

At least we can see, Pig encouraged. *You don't want to trip again.*

Trip again and get properly swallowed this time. It was not a welcome thought.

They took cover behind a boulder near the western edge of the compound fence and surveyed the scene before them. Insects thrummed close by. The black shadow of a bird glided above. Torches flickered in the king's residence and in a couple of the huts in the courtyard. Two guards holding spears stood outside the gate further along.

"Can you smell Grandpa Woe?" Pearly whispered.

No. Only trouble. Pig sounded unusually edgy.

"Any other guards?"

No. Just those ones. And some inside the huts.

That's when it started again. The ground trembled and a low rumbling noise rose through the earth below them. The night rumbles! Pearly looked back at the village huts, witnessing the swift dousing of the remaining torches. She felt a pang for the villagers. It must be terrifying for this to happen night after night and not understand why.

Pearly found Pig's eyes. They nodded at each other, then skulked out from their hiding spot and crept to the enormous pillar of rock that butted up against the compound fence. It was probably the tallest of all the rocky fingers and rose into the night sky, statuesque and menacing. It made Pearly's knees go weak. Thick clumps of bamboo surrounded the column, acting like an extension of the fence, leaving no obvious gap between it and the dense jungle. Snake-like vines twisted around the column and strands of feathery moss fell from the vines like a deep green waterfall. And below her the earth rumbled.

Pearly took a long breath and pushed through the bamboo, her machete at the ready. If Grandpa Woe

143

had gone this way, he certainly hadn't left any trace.

Tension threaded through Pearly's body. Everything she feared during her daytime treks was magnified in this night-time jungle. The sound of her boots stepping on the mooshy leaf matter under foot ricocheted up into the canopy above, as if broadcasting her presence. She sheathed her machete and stood stock still – slashing would make too much noise.

Smoky bacon, Pearly, oinked Pig. *Come on.*

Pig was right. She had to get moving. She couldn't let her fears get in the way. She had to do everything she could to find Grandpa Woe and her parents. She needed them desperately.

But what if I can't find them? What if I never find them? The thought crashed through her like a wave. *Oh smoky bacon!* This was so hard. She shoved a clump of damp branches out of her way.

She couldn't let it happen.

No adventure too small, no challenge too great – that's what it said in the Adventurologists' Guild's charter, but this adventure felt far too great for Pearly. Every step she took was weighed down by the challenge of it and the awful, but very real possibility that she might fail – again.

She had come on this adventure to prove herself and all she was doing was making more trouble for her family. Would Grandpa Woe be missing now if she didn't follow Prince Tub into the jungle? And what good did that do? She hadn't got any useful information and she hadn't been able to warn her parents. She had failed at that too.

She turned sideways to pass through the narrow gaps between tree trunks, her adventure pack scraping against bark, catching on knobbly bits and sticky-out twigs. She ducked under low hanging vines. She stepped over roots and fallen logs, Pig following close behind.

Her skin crawled. Her heart ached. Her eyes teared up. But she kept on going.

There must be a reason Pig's ma urged them to search behind the compound – and that reason must have something to do with King Foom Chu, Prince Tub and their guards.

Finally, the jungle started to open up, the trees now sparsely spread across a scrubby clearing. The pair stepped carefully through long prickly grasses, Pearly wincing with every step. She kept her eyes peeled. Her ears alert – even though she had no idea what she was looking out for.

Pig had his snout to the ground.

He could detect something, Pearly could tell. "What is it?" she whispered.

Not sure.

Pearly stopped abruptly, sucking in her breath.

Something had caught her eye in the shadows ahead. "Look," she whispered and then hurried off to investigate. "It's a track." Pearly knelt beside a wide ribbon of orange dirt. She pulled her torch from the side pocket of her pack and flicked it over the dirt. "Pig, these look like tyre treads – from a truck or a vehicle of some kind." She quickly turned off her torch. How could that be? There were no vehicles in Anachak. There were no roads. Pig grunted beside her, his piggy eyes wide and glowing pink in the dark.

Humans, Pig sniffed, and shivered. *It's faint but humans have been through here. Recently. Maybe even Prince Tub. And maybe ...*

"Maybe who?"

Maybe ... maybe Grandpa Woe. But I can't be certain. It's just a slight whiff. A hint.

The blood rushed to Pearly's head. She stood on shaky legs.

"Come on, then. I guess we better follow this track," she whispered, with fake bravado.

She was not feeling the slightest bit brave. Inside, she was convincing herself in Italian that the track was going to lead them right into the gaping, sharp-toothed mouth of trouble.

Grossi guai. Big trouble.

And she was right.

CHAPTER 24

They hadn't gone far along the wide dirt track when it started to curve and dip sharply, becoming stony. Instinctively, Pearly and Pig slowed their pace.

Pearly's ankle throbbed on the steep descent. Her boots slipped and crunched noisily on the gravelly dirt, each step announcing their arrival. But their arrival to where? Where was the track taking them? Pearly couldn't even begin to imagine.

Soon the track narrowed, and they were confined on either side by sheer rock walls. Was she entering a rocky gully or gorge? Pearly couldn't tell in the dark – and it was definitely getting darker. The overhanging branches of the trees above had stolen the moonlight.

Pearly slowed down even more. The sound of the earth grumbling and rumbling had started up again. It was faint at first, but the further into the steep gully they descended, the louder it became.

"I don't like this," Pearly hissed.

Pig ran his snout from side to side. *Neither do I*, he oinked, and started AROOing softly.

Strong scent of humans, Pig oinked suddenly. *Many. Prince Tub and ... yes ... Grandpa Woe!*

Grandpa Woe had been here! Pig's ma was right. Pearly hugged Pig, excitement and trepidation mingling in her gut. It was great they were getting close to Grandpa Woe, but why had he come here and why was Prince Tub here too? Too many questions and still no answers.

Pearly pushed herself up and steadied herself. Ahead, it seemed as though they were heading into some sort of dark tunnel – that gaping sharp-toothed mouth of Pearly's earlier imaginings.

A shudder ripped through her, as a new thought struck.

A gaping mouth? A mouth of a *cave* perhaps?

That actually made sense. The whole reason Grandpa Woe came to Anachak way back in the eighties, and the many times since, was to explore the extensive limestone cave systems in the area. Grandpa Woe had said that he didn't know about any caves in this part of the kingdom, but he did mention that the rock pillars reminded him of limestone stalagmites – which are usually found in caves. The dots were starting to join up. Perhaps Grandpa Woe had learned about some new cave when he caught up with his old pals and then decided to go to have a look. Or perhaps he had worried that Pearly had fallen into a cave pit or had gone exploring herself and got lost in the cave.

But what about the other humans and Prince Tub? Why would they be here if Grandpa Woe was looking for her and Pig? Or had just gone exploring?

She didn't know the answers to any of these questions, but she did know one thing for certain. They were getting closer to Grandpa Woe, and so they had to keep going, the need to find him an ache burning deep within her.

The rumbling is coming from inside, Pig noted.

Pearly stopped and listened. The rumbling was definitely funnelling out through the dark cave mouth they were approaching.

I can smell petrol fumes, he added.

Pearly sniffed. Pig was right about this too, and you didn't need a supersonic sniffer to smell it. The rumbling had to be an engine of a vehicle, but what was a vehicle doing in a limestone cave in the middle of the jungle in the almost forgotten kingdom of Anachak? It made no sense at all. The dots that Pearly had been joining broke apart.

They were finally at the cave entrance. Pearly pressed her back up against the rock wall, trying to dissolve into it. Pig hid behind her knees. The rumbling was blaringly loud here. The smell of petrol so strong,

Pearly could taste it. If there was a vehicle in there, it had to be one big cave, that's for sure, which wasn't that surprising; Grandpa Woe had told her many stories about the enormous caves in Anachak, with chambers as large as cathedrals and filled with thousands of hanging bats. But a vehicle had to be driven by somebody, which meant they were getting very close to being face-to-face with someone – probably one of the guards, or even Prince Tub himself. Whoever it was, she had to make sure they didn't see her or Pig. Somehow, they had to get past the vehicle, so they could explore inside and find her grandfather.

Easy! A walk in the park.

Not.

Pearly listened carefully to the droning engine noise, trying to work out where it was and what it might be doing. The noise seemed to fluctuate, like the ebb and flow of waves at the beach. "It sounds like it is going back and forth," she said to Pig.

Pig poked his head out and listened too. *Yes*, he oinked. *It comes and goes, comes and goes.*

Pearly waited until the rumbling noise started to retreat. She bent over and, keeping low and close to the shadow of the cave wall, crept inside. It was more like a tunnel than a cave, but they had only made it a few metres inside when the rumbling noise started to approach them. They both shrugged into the wall.

Once the noise started to recede, they crept further into the pitch black of the tunnel. When the noise started to return, they stopped again. This went on for some time, until finally Pearly could sense that they were close to where the vehicle was doing whatever it was doing. The tunnel at this point had a sharp bend. She crouched beside Pig and leant out to look around it.

What she saw made her gasp and fling herself back against the wall.

What's wrong? Pig oink-whispered.

Pearly didn't reply. She had to see it again to make sure she hadn't imagined it. She peeked around the bend again and took a long look at the scene in front of her, before sliding back.

"Pig," she said, breathless with the excitement of her discovery. "This isn't a cave. I think ... I think it's the lost city. I think we've found Mu Savan!"

CHAPTER 25

Pearly sat with her pack against the tunnel wall. She held her knees tight, as she tried to make sense of what she had seen. Pig stuck his head around the corner to see for himself.

Pearly catalogued the scene methodically in her mind. It was definitely a building. A large room or hall. Cut stone walls. Decorated columns. At least two wooden doors and another tunnel leading off. A couple of mounds of rubble and a tiled stone floor. Torches flamed all around, lighting up the space, revealing a noisy, spluttering, rumbling forklift truck carrying a load of wooden crates. A man and a woman were leaning into an open crate across the room. Another vehicle, perhaps an old-fashioned digger of some sort, was near the entrance, and there was ... gold! Gold glimmering everywhere. Especially on a large statue of a pig on a slab of rock in the centre of the room. The Sacred Statue of the Divine Sow!

Woozers! I think you could be right, Pig oinked. *It could well be Mu Savan. But with all the activity in there, I don't think the city is lost. It is definitely found.*

A lost city not lost. A lost city right beside the new Ban Noa. What was going on? King Foom Chu must know about this. He must know that the night rumbles were being made by the noisy old forklift and that digger, yet he let his people believe it was the Balance being disturbed. He knew Mu Savan was here, and the Sacred Statue of the Divine Sow too, yet he allowed her parents to trek off into the jungle to find it. Nothing made sense. Her brain felt as if it was filled with scrambled egg.

But there was one thing that was as clear as an alpine stream but as dangerous as a bubbling pool of lava. King Foom Chu was up to no good. Grandpa Woe was on the mark when he told her not to trust him.

"What can you smell?" Pearly whispered.

Pig edged his snout out from the tunnel wall and took three long sniffs.

He pulled back in, snorted and shook himself. A sure sign that what he had sniffed worried him.

Petrol fumes. But also humans. Prince Tub nearby. But others too. A puzzling mix of human scents – and some far away. He pushed his snout out again and had another sniff. *I am pretty sure I can smell Grandpa Woe, but Pearly, there's something else.* Pig paused and held Pearly's questioning gaze. *Don't get too worked up, okay?* Pearly nodded automatically. *Stay calm, promise?* Pearly chewed her bottom lip. *I think ... I can smell your parents!*

He added the last part so swiftly, it took Pearly a few moments to work out what he said. *Her parents? Pig could smell her parents?* Pearly blinked back tears. Large wet sobs rose in her throat. She tried to choke them down, but it was not possible. They rose up and out.

Pig snuggled against her. *I'm not sure, but I think I can smell Angel's shampoo and your dad's boots – they're quite stinky.*

"I don't know if it is a good thing or a bad thing," Pearly wondered out loud through her tears. "But at least we know they haven't been swallowed by the jungle." Relief washed over her. She hadn't realised how worried she had been.

She wiped her cheeks, then ran her fingers across her scalp and tugged at her curls with both hands. She didn't know what to do. Again. Her family were so close. And probably in need of help. But a forklift, a digger, Prince Tub and his guards and who else knew what stood between her and her family.

"What do we do now?" she asked Pig.

Pig grunted and scratched behind his ear with his trotter, thinking.

Pearly yanked off her pack and hugged it against her stomach, thinking.

Her mind went straight to the *RAG*. Grandpa Woe had written it for a reason. As a guide to help Adventurologists on their adventures. Surely, she could find something to help her within its pages.

She mentally flipped through the chapters, searching for some germ of advice that would help her hatch a plan. But stuck in the dark of a long tunnel, it all seemed devastatingly unhelpful.

Most of the basics were about planning and being prepared and following your passions and knowing your limits. This was not a time for following one's passions and she was all too aware of her limits – in fact, knowing her limits was the core of her problems. She really needed to ignore her limits, or she would never find her family.

She visualised the page on "Surviving Sticky Situations", mentally checking each point one by one. It was too late for number 7 – *don't panic* – because she was already panicking. And number 9 – *expect the unexpected* – only made her panic more. *Everything* around that bend was unexpected. What else might she find in there? Number 4 was good advice – *make the impossible possible* – but how? She was in an impossible situation, but how was she going to make finding her family possible? She groaned with frustration. *Sheesh,*

*Grandpa Woe, some practical examples wouldn't go astray! S*he needed to talk to Grandpa Woe about updating the *RAG*. If she could find him, that is.

The sound of the approaching forklift cranked up. Pearly's breath caught in her throat. Pig AROOed softly, the hairs on his back bristling. It sounded as if it was heading right for them. Was it leaving? Pearly leapt up, hooked her pack over one shoulder and looked about for a place to hide. There was none.

"Run!" she yelled to Pig.

They ran.

But they had only taken a few loping steps when the engine spluttered and puttered and then stopped. Pearly and Pig stopped too. They looked at each other. It was pin-drop quiet.

Pearly padded back to the bend in the tunnel, took a calming breath, then slid one eye out from the edge. The forklift had stopped right in front of her at the tunnel entrance. Pearly stretched her neck up and out to see over it. She caught a glimpse of the driver wandering off further into the large stone room, and then disappearing down what looked like a passageway. A quick scan of the rest of the room revealed that it was empty.

Number 6 from "Surviving Sticky Situations" flashed urgently in her head – *act quickly and decisively*.

Pearly ducked down and swivelled round to face Pig. "Come on, Pig," she said. "We're going in."

CHAPTER 26

With barely a moment's hesitation, Pearly followed by Pig scampered to the forklift, and went to ground behind it. Pearly's heartbeat was so loud she was sure her heart had abandoned her chest to find a new home behind her ears. She breathed in slowly through her nose and out through her mouth like Grandpa Woe had shown her. It's what he said he did whenever a passage in a cave looked too narrow or too difficult.

In through the nose and out through the mouth, then off you go. Grandpa Woe's wise words scooted through her head. She had to get to him – and hopefully her parents.

Pig sniffed. *The humans are all down that way – in that passageway,* he whisper-oinked.

"All of them?" Pearly whispered back.

All.

This was not the situation they needed. This was a worst-case scenario. But Pearly wouldn't let herself be deterred. *No challenge too great*, she reminded herself. She peeked over the top of the forklift cabin and surveyed the room, *assessing her risks*, as "Adventurologing – the basics" had taught her, and hoping that her three years of training would kick in. She mapped a route across the cavernous room to the wall beside the hallway: the forklift to the digger to the stack of crates to the left to behind the Sacred Statue to the pile of rocks on the right then to the wall. The longest and riskiest section being from the statue to the pile of rocky rubble. But she would worry about that when she got there, because right now it was time to *push her limits* and *act quickly and decisively*. Before her courage left her.

"Follow me," she told Pig, as she slunk out from the forklift, bolted to the digger, stooping over, muttering *act quickly and decisively*, over and over in Italian.

The two vehicles were only about two metres apart, but to Pearly it felt like a hundred. She leant against the digger to catch her breath.

Where next? asked Pig. *Those crates?*

Pearly nodded, and crept out. She crouch-ran. Pig flew past her, and then the two were behind the stack of four wooden crates. So far so good.

Pig put his nose to the crates. Pearly tried to peer through the gaps.

Smells old – ancient. Mossy and mildewy, Pig oinked.

"There're some flashes of gold. Perhaps some statues or artefacts," Pearly added. Artefacts were not unexpected. Ancient cities and archaeological digs often uncovered artefacts, sometimes valuable ones. But why would they be in crates and stacked up as if they were getting ready to be shipped out? Pearly had no idea, and now was not the time to ponder it. Now was the time to get to the statue before one of the guards or Prince Tub made an appearance.

"Now to the statue," Pearly whispered.

Pig gulped. His eyes flickered as if he was blinking back tears. *The Sacred Statue of the Divine Sow*, Pig oinked with awe.

"Is that okay?" Pearly asked.

Sure, Pig grunted, husky-voiced. *No choice.*

Pig led the charge this time; Pearly scarpered close behind him. They dodged the large open crate beside the statue and hunkered behind the rock plinth where the Divine Sow stood, beneath her divine curly tail.

Even from this unfortunate angle, there was something quite wonderful about the statue. Pearly could feel it. It glowed – not just because it was made of gold, but because it had an energy about it. It radiated, like the sun, and made Pearly feel warm and humbled and in awe. Pig was affected by it too. He had his head down, as if bowing, his ears floppy over the black splotches around his eyes. He was making a gentle sound that Pearly had never heard him make before. It was almost an AROO, but without the stress.

"What are you saying?" Pearly mouthed.

Just paying my respects, Pig replied.

Pearly scratched her head. She didn't really understand, but she didn't want to take away from Pig's moment. It obviously meant a lot to him to be so near this statue. But they couldn't stay here forever.

"Ready, Pig? The pile of rubble next. Okay?"

Pig nodded.

"Let's go then."

Pearly zeroed her focus on the mound of rocks and made a run for it. This was the most dangerous stretch – the one that had her exposed to view from the passageway the whole way. Her pulse pounded in her ears again. Her legs felt so unsteady she felt as if they might betray her. Finally, she was just a few steps shy, so she dived behind the heap.

"Phew," she said to Pig.

But Pig was not there. Pearly bent out. *Mamma mia!* He was still at the statue.

"Pig!" Pearly hissed across the room. "Pig!"

Pig was transfixed, staring up at the Divine Sow.

"PIG!" Pearly hissed louder this time.

That seemed to do the trick. A shudder jolted right through him. He shook his head as if to snap out of his trance and looked to Pearly.

160

But the expression on his face sent a jolt racing through her.

Pig was gawking at her with wide-eyed terror.

Pearly! Behind you! he warned.

But the warning came too late. Because behind her was Prince Tub, two guards and three spearheads pointing right at her.

CHAPTER 27

"Get up," Prince Tub Chu commanded in Anachakan, as one of the guards rounded up Pig to join her.

Pearly stood on legs that were almost too weak to hold her upright. One of the guards grabbed her to stop her from keeling over.

"Thank you, Pearly Woe," Prince Tub said, which was not at all what Pearly expected to hear. He was still wearing his orange sarong, but with a flowing blue shirt hanging over it. "You were my next problem. But you have now solved that problem for me," he continued, smiling an oily, not-to-be trusted smile. Pearly had no idea what he was talking about, but she knew too well that being a problem was never good. Pearly was an expert at being a problem. "Take them to join the others. A family reunion. How special."

The guard let go of Pearly and gave her a shove towards the passageway. As she stumbled forwards, she glanced behind her to see another guard prodding

Pig's rump with her spear. Pig shot the guard a scathing look and started AROOing loudly.

The passageway was long and narrow and dimly lit with a torch about halfway down and another some distance away. Chunks of timber shored up the tumbledown walls and ceiling and there was evidence of new stonework. Pearly stumbled along on the uneven stone floor, her ankle smarting again, her body sore and oh-so-tired. Pig's AROOing echoed through the narrow space and bounced all around her. It was comforting and distressing all at once.

They passed by the first torch, its black smoke tickling Pearly's nose. She studied the section of stonework around it, lit golden and flickering by the torch flame. It seemed intact and original. Grey and mildewy, but also elaborately carved with pig motifs, banana trees, curling jungle vines and jagged mountain peaks. Mu Savan – which Pearly was now certain this indeed was – must have been a wonderful, beautiful, rich city in its day, whenever that was.

The guards marched Pearly and Pig all the way to the end of the passageway, where the last torch blinked beside a hefty wooden door, guarded by two men. Elaborately carved ancient stone surrounded the door on all three sides, but the door itself seemed much more recent, and was bolted across by two solid planks of wood that slotted into stone hooks on either side.

With a loud grunt, the guards slid the wooden planks out of the hooks. They placed them on the ground beside the door, then one guard jiggled a long rusty key into an old-fashioned lock on the door. He demanded Pearly hand over her pack and then thrust her roughly into the dark gloom of the room, along with a grunting and irritated Pig. Pearly landed sprawled out on the stone floor, the foul smell of human waste and body odour making her gag. Before the door closed, she glimpsed a couple of sleeping bodies and three shocked faces.

Shocked faces that she knew so well!

"Pearly!" Her mother pounced and wrapped her arms around her, kissing her on the head over and over. "Oh Pearly, are you okay?"

Her father joined the hug. "Pearly, we've been beside ourselves."

Pig grunted to remind everyone of his presence. "Pig!" shouted Angel. "You found Pig." Angel reached over and drew Pig into the hug too. Pearly was relieved, but also distraught. It was so wonderful to be reunited with her family, but she was painfully aware that they were all locked in what looked like a dungeon.

"Where were you?" A scratchy voice rose out of the dark. "I looked everywhere, and you had vanished." Grandpa Woe!

Pearly pulled free from her parents' arms and

wiggled over to where Grandpa Woe was sitting propped up against the stone wall.

She huddled close to him. "I'm sorry, Grandpa Woe. I saw Prince Tub follow Mum and Dad. I was just going to have a quick look to see what he was doing, but then I saw him take down their red tree markers and so I waited till he moved on and replaced them, so Mum and Dad could find the way home."

"You did what?" Her father gripped his head with both hands. "That was so dangerous, Pearly."

Pearly was shocked at her father's reaction – but then she realised she shouldn't have been. "I ... I ..." she stammered. "I only did what you or Mum would do ... what the *RAG* says to do. I acted decisively. I was getting information ... I ..." She couldn't win with her father.

"That might be so," countered her father. "But it was also dangerous. This whole adventure was such a mistake."

"There was no way for us to know about Foom Chu," said her mother. "The adventure wasn't a mistake, it just hasn't gone to plan."

"That's an understatement," whispered Grandpa Woe. "Now finish your story, Pearly."

Ricky rubbed the back of his neck and hung his head.

Pearly wiped her eyes. "I didn't know whether I should keep following," she continued, "or go back and tell you, Grandpa Woe, but then I tripped and tumbled down a cliff–"

"A cliff?" Her father's voice from the dark. "You could have been killed or ..."

"Ricky ..." warned her mother.

"I'm *fine.*" Pearly almost hissed the word. "I'm just bruised and my ankle is sore. But it was dark and I didn't know how to get back. I'm sorry that I disappeared on you, Grandpa Woe."

And she *was* sorry. But as she put voice to her story, she was also confused. She had done what any Adventurologist would do, hadn't she? She had stepped boldly into the jungle like her parents, but somehow it was still wrong.

There was some movement and rustling from the direction of the sleeping bodies. Pearly's eyes had adjusted to the dark now and she could make out two men and a young woman stretching and pushing themselves up to sit. More prisoners?

"Pearly, Pig," said Grandpa Woe. "Let me introduce you to my good friend, King Alung Chu, his son and daughter, Prince Keej and Princess Jong."

Shock shot onto Pearly's face. Pig kicked his legs with surprise.

"You're not swallowed?" said Pearly.

King Alung Chu laughed a deep belly laugh, scratching at his long grey beard, as Prince Keej stretched and yawned, and Princess Jong reached across and rubbed Pig's back.

"No, the jungle did not swallow us," said King Alung Chu. "Mu Savan did – we've been imprisoned in its belly for many months now. And sadly my brother is the culprit. He is bringing great shame to our family and causing much pain for my people." The king's chin dropped to his chest. He was covered in grime and his ribs stuck out like a bony cage, his chest hollow. He had only a few wiry wisps of grey hair stuck across his head and a few more hanging from his chin.

"Your brother's actions are not your shame," Grandpa Woe said, with genuine affection. "He alone owns that."

"Thank you, Gordon. My brain understands this, but my heart cannot accept it. Especially now that Foom has brought such hardship on the Woes. Family to the people of Anachak."

"We are honoured to be part of the Chu family and it will be our honour to help to restore you as king and to stop Foom Chu's reign."

"I do not know ... how ... that can be ... possible," said Prince Keej, in faltering English. He too was covered in grime, but was muscly and strong. "I am sorry my English is ... how did you say it, Gordon? Crusty?"

"I think I said rusty, but crusty works," Grandpa Woe said. "We've been speaking mainly English,

Pearly, in case there are prying ears around. I taught the king English when I stayed with him all those years back and he taught me Anachakan. And the prince and princess both spent a year each in an English-speaking school in Thailand."

"It is good to practise," said the prince. "The mind becomes boggy in here. Nothing to do and escape impossible."

"The Woes are Adventurologists, Prince Keej," said Pearly's mother who had crawled up beside Pearly and had one arm firmly around Pearly's shoulder. "And we are expert at making the impossible possible. We train for it."

"We do indeed," chimed in Pearly's father. "And there is no way we are going to spend more time than necessary in this dungeon. So we need a plan."

"And to plan," said Grandpa Woe, "we need information. *Knowledge is power.* So, now that Pearly's here, let's pool our knowledge. Share our stories. And together we will find a way."

Pearly slumped back against the stone wall and thought about what she had discovered on her way here and her heart plummeted.

Getting out of here was yet another impossible task.

A hopeless situation.

The type she seemed to excel in.

CHAPTER 28

In the stinky gloom of their stone prison, the captives sat in a circle on the damp floor to gather information.

King Alung Chu sat beside Pig and scratched his hide. "It makes my heart glad and my eyes happy to see Pig again." Pearly was impressed with the king's command of English. His smile was broad and full-faced, the wrinkle lines around his eyes breaking layers of dried muck into semicircles of happiness.

Princess Jong coaxed Pig onto her lap. Pig was all too willing, to Pearly's mind, and he curled up contentedly, almost purring as the young princess ran her hand along his back, saying, "*Chu-la! Chu-la! Chu-la!*" *Pig! Pig! Pig!* in a high-pitched gush that set Pearly's teeth on edge.

The princess was at least ten years younger than her brother. Pearly guessed that she was maybe fourteen or fifteen at the most. She too was skinny and grubby from her long months locked away, but beneath the grime and the wild knotted hair, Pearly could see she had bright eyes and a beaming smile.

The loud rumbly grumble of spluttering vehicles in the chamber started up again, making the earth vibrate. It was a fair distance away, but the prison room seemed to capture the sound and bounce it off all four walls. It was an ominous sound. Pearly didn't like it.

King Alung Chu launched into the story of how they had discovered the ruins of Mu Savan – a tale that had her father's eyes open wide and reaching for his notebook, only to curse when he remembered he no longer had it.

The king told how the discovery of Mu Savan was made about five years ago after an earthquake. One of the villagers had been out foraging a few days later and had come across some unusual stone slabs that had become visible after the earth shifted. When the Chu family investigated, they discovered that the fingers of rock that were entwined with creepers and roots and tree trunks were indeed the stone pillars of the temple that housed the Sacred Statue of the Divine Sow. They set out to clear the jungle around the area and discovered a few sink holes that led them underground to where the city had been buried centuries ago. Some rooms were intact. Others were nothing more than ruins. But importantly the chamber with the Sacred Statue was almost completely untouched and the statue in perfect condition as it had been for centuries.

"Can you imagine our immense joy," King Alung Chu said, running his fingers across his scalp, "when we made these discoveries, and started to repair and shore up the ruins? The whole village was uplifted and united – and so excited. They were happy days."

"So what went wrong?" her father asked. He had been hanging off the king's every word.

"Ultimately, my brother's greed, but at first it was that we realised how this discovery could change the way we have lived in Anachak. Now that Mu Savan was no longer lost, we risked being 'discovered', plus there were great riches to be found buried throughout. We had lived with anonymity, almost forgotten, for all this time, and we wanted it to stay that way. The countries around us are too busy, too modern, too complicated for us. Many do not respect the river or the jungle."

Pearly bit on her bottom lip, her brow scrunched together as she listened to the king tell his sad tale, his words thick with the betrayal and humiliation of being holed up in this dungeon for so long.

"Is that why you moved the village?" Angel asked.

"Yes," chimed in Prince Keej. He frowned in concentration as he searched for the right English words. "We needed to make a ... shield for Mu Savan ... to ..."

"Protect it?" Pearly tried.

"Yes – to protect it. So we protected it by hiding it right in the eyes of everyone."

Pearly pondered on this one for a bit before she understood. "Oh, in plain sight!"

"Yes, in eyesight of everyone. We make our village right over the top of it. It was a sun-bright plan."

"That was my brother's plan, as you probably guessed." Princess Jong laughed as she scratched between Pig's ears. "He likes to boast."

King Alung Chu took over the telling. "The whole village became the protectors then, and we were able to look after the ruins and the statue as part of our daily life. And my son is right – it was a brilliant plan."

Pearly sat bolt upright with a sudden realisation. The villagers knew! They knew that Foom Chu was lying to her family – sending them off on a useless trek to find a city that was not lost. Were they that scared of Foom Chu that no one dared to breathe a word to them?

"The jungle did the rest," Prince Keej added. "It quickly gobbled the buildings of the old village and made the jungle tracks go into the air."

"The bananas," Pearly said, remembering the great piles of bananas scattered throughout the old Ban Noa. "Did you put them there?"

The princess laughed again. "That one was my

idea. The bananas attracted the macaques and the macaques became so banana obsessed, they scared off any curious visitors who might threaten their supply. Hey, how did you get past them?"

"Pearly," said Grandpa Woe. "She has a gift. She can communicate with animals. She calmed them and even got them to tell us where the new village was."

This got them talking about language and animals, and Pig and the poisoning of Pig's ma.

"What a disgrace," thundered King Alung Chu. He got up and stalked around the dark room, pulling at the fine wires of his beard and waving his arms around as he spoke. "She is our living Divine Sow. A direct descendant of the first Divine Sow. We need her to produce a new sow before it is her time. What was my foolish brother thinking?"

"Come sit, Alung," Grandpa Woe said. "We need to keep level-headed. Foom is all about creating fear. He has your people so fearful, they won't venture out of their huts, let alone into the jungle. They believe you have been swallowed by the jungle itself. He has the machinery going at night and tells them that it is the earth rumbling because the Balance has been disturbed and the Divine Sow displeased."

"He is the one disturbing the Balance." The king's words were wound tight with anger.

"What does he want?" asked Ricky.

"He wants to get rich and live in a city palace, that's what he wants," answered the king, who had not sat as Grandpa Woe had requested. He stood, hands on hips, fury on his face. "He wants everything that we have sought to avoid. He was pressuring me to sell some artefacts and allow him to bring in diggers and other equipment to dig out the collapsed walls so he could locate all the statues and gold and artefacts and then sell them too. When I refused, and said it was not the way of the Anachakans, that we wanted a simple life where the river and jungle provided, he lured us down through the secret passage in our residence and locked us up."

"He's not planning to keep you here forever, is he?" mumbled Pearly, her eyes downcast staring at the stone floor, her brow furrowed. "And us too?"

"No. I think not. He will gather all the valuables and take off with them. Then I presume he will let us go. We may be living in foul conditions, but we are fed and given fresh water each day. He means us no harm; he is just greedy."

"We have belief he is almost ready – so you arriving would have walked up his nostrils," added the prince.

Pearly clamped her lips shut to stop a giggle escaping.

"Is the Sacred Statue still in place?" the king asked urgently.

Pig started muttering his soft in awe way of

AROOing at the mention of the statue. Princess Jong snuggled her cheek against his side, cooing into his ears.

"Yes," said Pearly, through clenched teeth, looking sideways at the princess. "But there is a large open crate beside it."

The king groaned, as if in great pain. "It is as I feared," he said. "Foom is almost ready to leave."

At this point, the group concentrated on gathering information about what was happening outside. Grandpa Woe told how he went looking for Pearly the night she went missing and ended up finding the same road as Pearly into the hidden city. Pearly relayed all she could remember about the landscape around the tunnel and the thickness of the jungle from her approach.

Angel and Ricky told them how eventually they had noticed Prince Tub following them, and so they decided to lead him in the opposite direction to where they were planning to go, but had ended up right on top of another entrance to the north.

"I couldn't believe my eyes when I located what at first seemed like a rocky crevasse," Ricky said, "but it was actually a shaft with a bamboo ladder."

"We took the ladder down," Angel said, rubbing at her eyes and yawning, "but the prince saw us and followed us, and that's how we ended up here."

"It was quite the journey through a labyrinth of tunnels," Ricky continued, catching Angel's yawn. "I don't think we could find our way back out."

"The mountain to climb is this dungeon," said Prince Keej. "There is no way out. We have tried."

The first rays of soft morning light drifted through the narrow slatted opening high on the far wall. They were all too weary to continue, so that's how they left it. A problem – or a mountain climb – to mull over.

It was certainly a problem.

A problem that didn't have an obvious solution.

Pearly lay uncomfortably on the stone floor. Pig was already pig-snoring, curled up between her and Princess Jong.

Pearly couldn't sleep though, her mind was whirring with images of explorers years from now stumbling upon Mu Savan, and finding this very dungeon and the dry-boned skeletons of seven humans and one pig.

CHAPTER 29

Pearly woke stiff and sore and downcast. How were they ever going to get out of this dungeon? How were they ever going to be able to make the impossible possible? Was it possible that this impossible was far too impossible to turn around? It would be like trying to turn around a gigantic ocean tanker in a narrow river. There was simply no way to do it.

She surveyed the room with one eye open. Even in the daylight, the room was shadowy. It seemed everyone was still asleep. King Alung Chu, Grandpa Woe and Angel were having a competition to see who could snore the loudest.

Pearly sighed. She couldn't imagine staying here one day, let alone months. The Chus had suffered greatly at the hands of their own family. It was a disgrace.

Footsteps sounded outside. The scrape and clang of the wooden planks being lifted up and out of their hooks roused the rest of the group, and by the time the lock jangled and the door opened, the grimy band of prisoners were propping themselves up, yawning and stretching and rubbing their eyes.

Two men entered carrying a large pot and a basket with bananas, mangoes and green-skinned melons. The aroma of coconut and fish eddied in with them. Pearly's stomach gave a tiger growl. Another had a bucket of water, and a basket with cups and bowls. The fourth brought in an empty bucket and took away the smelly toilet bucket from behind the bamboo screen, the content sloshing around as he walked. Pearly put her hands over her mouth and nose. The two dungeon guards stood at the doorway holding their spears in front of them.

The men dropped their wares and then hotfooted it out. The whole operation took less than a minute. Six people to deliver food – and done in a way that provided no chance of escape.

Prince Keej looked into the pot. "Fish soup with coconut and rice noodles." He licked his lips.

"Phew," said Princess Jong. "I was sure it'd be wild boar again." Pig squealed in distress at the mention of eating a relative. "I'm sorry," she crooned, stroking his back tenderly. "That was insensitive, but I can't get used to you being able to understand human language."

Pig closed his eyes, head on his trotters, savouring the back rub.

Pearly changed the topic. "That coconut is making my mouth water."

"Dig up!" said the prince cheerily.

"Dig *in*," corrected Grandpa Woe and patted his back.

"The food is very good." The king handed out the bowls. "As I said, Foom means us no harm. But there will be no more until tomorrow. I suggest a small bowl now while it's warm, and then another later. The fruit will help to stop the boredom of the day."

Pearly's father stretched. He tucked in his shirt and dusted off his trousers. "No boredom today. Today we plan our escape. Dig up!" he added playfully.

Dig in or dig up, Pearly didn't care. She was famished, and King Alung Chu was right – the soup was delicious. She used her fingers to pick out the chunks of white fish and to hook the slippery rice noodles that seemed harder to snare at times than wiggly worms. She drank the soup directly from the bowl. Pig devoured his in seconds, snout in the bowl, licking every last bit.

Angel was packing away the bowls and cups and Grandpa Woe was moving the large pot out of the way, when something struck Pearly on the back of her head.

She clutched at her head and turned around. A banana lay on the ground behind her. "Who threw the banana?" She looked around at the bemused faces.

"What are you taking about?" said her father.

Pearly picked up the banana and held it up. "This just hit me on the head."

"You must have imagined it, sweetie," said her mother, just as Princess Jong yelped, "Ouch," and held a hand to her head too. Another banana lay on the ground.

"Keej, you're a grown man. You are too old to play these silly games," said the princess.

"Me? Why would I throw bananas?" protested the prince.

They all looked at each other, bewildered, as a banana fell from the sky and hit Grandpa Woe on his faded orange hat.

Pearly tilted her head back to study the slatted opening high above her. And to the astonishment of the Chu family, she slapped her arms against her sides, and called out, ARR-ARR OO-OO, ARR-ARR OO-OO, WAR-WARR! which was monkey for, *Wah-Wah! Wah-Wah, is that you?*

She waited for a moment then slapped her sides and called out again, *Wah-Wah! I know you're there.*

And he was. A furry little elfish face with pointy ears and golden eyes appeared at the opening. He pushed his face up against the slats and then tossed in another banana – this time clonking the king on the shoulder.

Wah-Wah jumped up and down on the window ledge screeching with laughter.

That's not funny, Pearly told him. *You just hit the king.*

Wah-Wah shrugged. *King likes bananas.* Wah-Wah hooked his arm around one of the stone slats and hung from it. *Jungle line say you stuck in here. So I come to save the banana head. You need saving too much!* the cheeky monkey scolded.

"What's he saying?" Angel asked.

"The jungle line told him we were here. He's come to save us," Pearly said, without taking her eyes off Wah-Wah.

"What's this jungle line?" Her father stood beside her, neck stretched, brow furrowed.

"I'm not sure exactly. But I think all the jungle animals communicate somehow – pass messages on. It's how Wah-Wah told me you and Mum weren't in the jungle any more."

"It is true," said the king. "The jungle looks after itself and helps those who look after it."

"Rather hard to believe, isn't it?" said her father.

"And a girl talking to monkeys and pigs is totally believable?"

"Point taken."

"How will the monkey save us?" Princess Jong eased Pig off her lap and joined the others below the window.

181

Pearly held her arms out, palms up, and made the noises that asked the princess's question. *How can you save us?*

Wah-Wah screeched and chittered and lobbed down three more bananas. Then he said, *Eat bananas. Bananas make you strong. When you are strong, I will bring help to save you.*

And with that the little monkey vaulted from the window edge and disappeared.

Pearly relayed Wah-Wah's words, and the seven prisoners were left scratching their heads (or his behind, in Pig's case), their mouths hanging open with shock.

Was it possible?

CHAPTER 30

Wah-Wah didn't return that day, or the next, which made Pearly bite her fingernails down to the quick. Had he deserted them?

Besides, how could a monkey help them anyhow? The prisoners had argued this point over and over, until it made Pearly's head ache. In the end it didn't matter whether they believed Wah-Wah or not, because they hadn't been able to come up with an alternative escape plan anyhow. So it was the monkey coming through for them, or they were stuck in this dark and smelly dungeon. Maybe forever.

King Alung Chu was getting increasingly frustrated as the activity in the chamber had escalated the night before and was even worse tonight. Tonight, they could hear Prince Tub yelling instructions and cursing – his stress levels mirroring the king's. And they all knew why.

And that "why" meant it wouldn't matter if Wah-Wah returned or not, because it was clear that Prince

Tub was in the process of trying to get the Sacred Statue of the Divine Sow off its stone plinth and into the crate. King Alung Chu was convinced that once that happened, Foom Chu and Tub and the rest of his family would leave with the statue and the other artefacts. This would be devastating for the people of Anachak, but he also firmly believed that the prisoners would then be released.

Pearly wasn't so sure about this last part. She didn't share King Alung Chu's belief that his brother wouldn't hurt them. He obviously didn't care about the people of Ban Noa. He was willing to have them live in fear. He imprisoned his own flesh and blood for months. Who knew what he would do when he fled with the loot?

Noises from the chamber boomed down the passageway.

The king pressed his forehead against the dungeon wall, the inevitability of what was about to happen making his body slump with the weight of it, his hollow chest heaving. Prince Keej rested one hand on his shoulder. Princess Jong huddled in a nearby corner, clutching Pig close, the princess's need for comfort taking some of the heat out of Pearly's jealousy. The Woes sat propped up against the back wall, shoulder to shoulder, Angel holding Pearly's hand.

No one spoke. The time for words had passed.

A loud shout jolted into the night air. "*Yool!*" which was Anachakan for "Heave!"

The tension in the dungeon tightened. King Alung Chu gasped. Pearly held her breath. Pig oinked, OINKY OINKY NO-NO! OINKY OINKY NO-NO!

Then again, "*Yool! Yool!*" followed by a sharp cracking, and a deep growl and crash, like a heavy swell pounding the coast.

Pig started AROOing. Pearly winced, her shoulders drawn up to her ears, her eyes closed. They all braced themselves. This was it.

But then it wasn't.

Instead of the grunt and groan of one final heave as the Divine Sow was lifted from her centuries-old plinth, the earth beneath them shook.

For real, this time – and not just from the sound of the underground vehicles.

It juddered and trembled and rocked. The earth was really moving. Dirt fell from the stone roof above them, showering them all. The Woes clutched each other, Angel muttering fearfully about Iceland and earthquakes. Pig scampered out of the princess's lap and joined the huddle. The princess dashed to be with her brother and father.

Screams and yells and the thudding of retreating, running feet ricocheted down the passageway.

Then silence.

King Alung Chu pushed himself off the wall. He ran his eyes around the dungeon. Then he straightened himself and said, "A tremor. A warning. The Sacred Statue of the Divine Sow has spoken. If Foom continues with this foolishness, we are all doomed and so is the Kingdom of Anachak. The earth will open and take us all. It will be the end."

Pearly brushed the dirt from her eyes and lips, and shook it out of her hair, all the while thinking, *Wah-Wah. Please, Wah-Wah. Time is running out. You are our only chance.*

The rest of the night was strangely, creepily quiet. No more tremors. No more shaking. No more earth moving beneath them. But also no more shouts or cursing or groans and no rumbly engine noises. Nothing. Only the sound of the breeze rattling through the jungle, and the occasional call of a night bird, or growl of a prowling animal. Pearly wondered if they had been left here to rot.

But right on schedule the next morning, four people entered carrying food and water and a new bucket. Two more stood guard. The stench of the toilet bucket left the dungeon as the aroma of spices and rice and fresh fruit drifted in. The dungeon door was closed and the planks clunked into place.

Another day locked away in this dungeon. Another day with no Wah-Wah and no chance of escape.

Pearly shovelled a handful of spicy rice into her mouth and looked around the room while she chewed. Princess Jong was peeling a mango for Pig. Again, Pig was almost purring with contentment, and Pearly was getting tired of it. Pig loved the princess's attention far too much. He was obviously smitten. And he certainly seemed to love Anachak. Who could blame him? This was where he was born. It was in his blood; it was his heritage. Pearly's chest fluttered. Would Pig want to return with them to Orchard Island when they escaped?

If they escaped, Pearly wondered miserably.

Pearly sensed this was the question on everyone's mind. No one had put voice to it, but it was starting to show. The king just snapped at Grandpa Woe, accusing him of taking too much rice, and Grandpa Woe snapped back, telling the king to mind his own beeswax. It was a tense moment as the two old friends faced off. The prince ignored the scene, his face grey and pinched. The princess rubbed at the dark circles around her eyes – she looked worn out. Ricky leant against the wall with his legs outstretched, sucking rice from his grubby fingers, his shirt untucked and undone, and his neck scarf round his head like a bandana. Pearly barely recognised him. And her mother had simply gone quiet. None of her usual long stories, just grunts, eyebrow raises with single word answers. She had barely spoken since the earth tremor last night.

Pearly didn't know how much longer they could take this. She remembered when she had followed Prince Tub and it had felt like she had a hive of worries thrumming through her, but now it felt as if her worries were Mount Everest high, and just as impossible to scale without oxygen, or a miracle. The thought made her queasy. She flicked the rice from her fingers and pushed her meal away.

Just then, something splashed into her bowl, knocking it over.

A banana! And another. It was raining bananas!

One, two, three, four, five, six, seven bananas flew in through the slatted window, landing *splat, splat, splat, splat, splat, splat, splat* on the ground.

Wah-Wah! Pearly could scarcely believe it. She eased herself off the floor, as that impish face appeared through the slats.

He chittered and squealed and squawked and waved his arms around.

Eat up, banana head, he squawked. *Need to be monkey strong.*

What are you planning? Pearly asked, her head thrown back, her neck stretching, fingers crossed behind her back. Maybe they had a chance to get out of this place!

Be ready, Wah-Wah squawked back.

For what? Pearly asked, panicked.

You'll see. This is monkey business. We know what to do.

And then he was gone.

Pearly turned to find everyone gawking at her.

"What did he say?" Grandpa Woe asked, scratching at the grubby stubble on his chin.

"He said to eat the bananas and be ready," Pearly replied.

"Be ready for what?" asked her father, his eyes wide and disbelieving.

"For ... monkey business?" Pearly mumbled. It sounded ridiculous, even to her.

King Alung Chu agreed. He crossed his arms across his chest and raised his chin in the air. "Preposterous. No monkey can save us. You felt the tremor. We are doomed. The Divine Sow is leaving, and when that happens it is the end."

"I don't know about that," said Grandpa Woe. "But I do think that monkey's eaten too many bananas!"

Pig grunted loudly then shot through Princess Jong's legs, making her gasp with surprise, scampered through the huddle and rushed to the door, snout to the ground.

Monkeys! Pig oinked. *I smell monkeys – macaques – hundreds of them!*

189

CHAPTER 31

Pearly raced to the door and squatted beside Pig. Pig looked at her, the thrill of his discovery shining in his pink eyes.

Can you hear them? he oinked.

Pearly put her ear to the door and listened hard. And there it was – a faint drumming sound way off in the distance, getting louder and closer. "I think I can."

"What's going on?" King Alung Chu demanded.

Pearly swivelled to face the king. "The monkeys are coming."

The king scowled at her at first, but the drumming became louder and he too put his ear to the door, along with Pearly.

Feet. Monkey feet. Hundreds of monkey feet galloping, rushing, charging. And screeching. Screaming. Roaring. A tidal wave of sounds heading their way. Filling the chamber and then funnelling down the passage.

The guards outside screamed. A scream that sent alarm racing through Pearly's veins. A great scuffle erupted in the passageway. The enormous racket of the storming macaques and the screams of the guards made Pearly put her hands over her ears and Angel put a protective arm over her shoulder.

Something thumped against the door. Another thump and another and then the tell-tale clang of the planks of wood being lifted out of their slots, followed by ear-piercing high-pitched screams.

Pearly tried to make out what the macaques were screaming. Demands. Threats. They wanted the door unlocked, but the guards didn't understand.

Pearly banged on the door. "UNLOCK THE DOOR!" she screamed in Anachakan. "THEY WANT YOU TO UNLOCK THE DOOR!"

The door shook as something thumped against it again. The monkeys screeched their demands louder, more insistent. Pearly yelled to the guards. And at last, the lock jangled.

"Step back!" ordered the king, just as the door flung open to reveal the guards sprawled out on the floor with macaques climbing all over them, and others snapping their spears in half.

The king ushered the prince and princess out the door. "Hurry! Follow me!" he added.

Ricky grabbed Pearly's hand and the two dashed

through the door, with Pig, Angel and Grandpa Woe close behind. They bolted down the passageway, the raiding monkeys screeching past them.

The king stopped at the end of the passageway and put both hands to his chest as he saw the Sacred Statue of the Divine Sow glowing golden in her place.

"Thank goodness," he breathed. He bowed low and then lurched into the chamber, pushing past the monkeys that continued to gallop inside, screeching and leaping about – a never-ending river of them. Pearly watched as a mob of monkeys herded two men and a woman past her and down the passageway towards the dungeon. The two guards were back on their feet and all five were shoved into the dungeon. Pearly gulped. These monkeys meant business.

"Come on, Pearly," urged her father, dragging her with him.

The king made a sharp right turn past the pile of rubble and to a closed wooden door. He turned to check they were all with him, before opening the door.

"This way," he shouted above the racket. But before he could enter, he was thrust aside by the screeching monkeys who tore into a new passageway, making the Woes and the Chus press themselves flat like human pizzas up against the back wall to avoid being trampled.

Pig burrowed in behind Pearly's knees to escape the stampede. His sides quivered against her calves.

Pearly's heart pounded her chest. The noise made her breathless. What had she started? Were the macaques taking over this Ban Noa too?

"Pearly, can you call them off?" yelled her father, panic in his voice, as he ducked out of the way of a large monkey leaping off one of the crates, then narrowly missing another bolting past.

Pearly didn't like her chances. She couldn't think straight, let alone speak Monkey. She opened her mouth, and a weak "*Ferma*," dribbled out, which was Italian for *Stop*, and not even Monkey. *Mamma mia! Smoky bacon!* She went to try again, when something plopped heavily on her shoulder, making her yelp instead.

A furry face rubbed against her own mucky one. Wah-Wah!

Make them stop, Pearly yelled, finally remembering how to speak Monkey.

Wah-Wah leant his face right into hers. *Why? They rescue you. They helping.*

But we are rescued now. What are they doing?

Silly, silly, banana head. Rescue not finished. This is monkey busines. Stay here until all monkeys inside. We know what to do.

Wah-Wah climbed onto her head and then launched himself into the throng of stampeding monkeys heading into the passage.

Pearly turned to the others, pressed against the wall, arms outstretched, their faces full of fear and questions.

"He said to stay here, until all the monkeys are gone," Pearly yelled.

"What are they doing?" shouted King Alung Chu. "The passageway leads into the Royal Compound!"

"Monkey business," Pearly shouted back, which didn't sound at all reassuring. "He said the rescue isn't finished."

The king didn't look too impressed. But they really had no choice; they were all pinned to the wall. One wrong move could see their heads taken out by the furry charge.

Pearly felt useless. This was her fault. Why did she trust Wah-Wah?

Pig must have felt her anxiety, because he rubbed his face against her legs, oinking loudly, *Smoky bacon to those worries. You've got this.*

She took in a long fearful breath of funky monkey-filled air. She hoped he was right.

At last, the tide of monkeys started to thin enough for them to step away from the wall.

Grandpa Woe scratched at his stubble and pulled his hat down low. "That was a first," he said and chuckled. He pulled Pearly close and whispered. "You did good, Pearly."

Pearly welcomed the praise, but she still wasn't convinced.

Prince Keej poked his head into the passageway. "All clear," he said, and stepped inside.

Pig followed, his snout to the ground.

Monkey scent everywhere, he oinked. *Human scent faint. Distant. Moving away.*

Pearly relayed this back to the others, as the band of escapees gingerly entered the passageway, the sound of the monkeys quite muffled now.

The passageway had a few twists and turns. It went through another smaller chamber and then into an even smaller room, which to the delight of the Woes had their adventure packs stacked against one wall. They quickly pulled them on.

It felt great to have her pack again; the familiar weight on Pearly's back was like a sign that maybe, just maybe, there was an end in sight.

She swivelled around to see Princess Jong push against a door, not dissimilar to the one to their dungeon.

"Through here," said King Alung Chu.

Grandpa Woe and Pig trotted through after the royals, Angel and Ricky waiting for Pearly to go in front of them. The door led to a steep stone staircase. It was night-time dark and their footsteps echoey as the screeches of the monkeys intensified with each step.

The stairs led to a trapdoor that the princess pushed open, bringing with it the enormous din of the macaques, who sounded as if they were in some kind of battle.

One by one they all climbed out.

Pearly pushed herself through the trapdoor, her thighs burning. She hauled herself out into a large living space in the king's residence.

She swallowed hard as she surveyed the scene before her. It was what she had feared.

The macaques, it seemed, had taken over the compound.

CHAPTER 32

The monkeys were everywhere. Hanging from the rafters. Swinging from beam to beam. Leaping from chair to table to bench. Charging from room to room. Knocking pots and bowls and pig statues over. Wreaking havoc. It was a scene of utter clamorous chaos.

King Alung Chu stood beside the secret staircase, his face screwed into a scowl, as his eyes slid around the large open space. "What are they doing to my compound?" he demanded, snaring Pearly with a look that made her knees weak. A look that laid the blame squarely on her, as if this was all her fault, which it probably was, and which only made it all the more difficult for her to stay upright.

"I ... er ... um ..." Pearly couldn't find a single word to explain.

"It's not Pearly's fault!" Ricky pushed past Pearly and approached the king, wagging his finger at him. Pearly's mouth fell open with surprise. "She is–"

Pearly didn't get to find out what her father was about to say because at that moment, Pig pushed his snout into Pearly's knees, and oinked, *Look! Foom Chu and Tub!*

Pearly looked to where Pig's snout was pointing. And there they were, scurrying out of the building – Foom trying to tie his sarong as he ran and Tub with three monkeys clinging to him. "King Foom and Prince Tub are escaping!" Pearly shouted.

Several other people ran screaming out into the compound too – members of Foom's family, Pearly guessed. Dozens of monkeys chased after them, snapping at their heels and launching onto their backs.

King Alung Chu squinted out of the doorway. "Tell the monkeys to stop them!" he shouted at Pearly.

Now he wants help! But it wasn't needed, because the monkeys had it under control. They knew monkey business and that monkey business was intent on herding Foom and Tub and the rest of his family and their guards into the centre of the compound, where five enormous elephants stood blocking their way out, the smashed remains of the gate and part of the compound fence littering the ground behind them. Samam stood proudly right in the middle.

"Samam!" Pearly cried.

"Another friend of yours?" the king asked, and Pearly nodded.

WARRR-ORR-WARRR! WARRR-ORR-WARRR! The elephants trumpeted and flapped their ears and stamped their feet. There was no escape for Foom Chu and his family and guards. They stood in the middle of the compound, surrounded by screeching, threatening, tail-waving, fang-baring monkeys and blocked by a great grey wall of trumpeting elephants, kicking up dust.

King Alung Chu pulled at his wiry beard and winked at Pearly. Then he strode into the compound. Prince Keej and Princess Jong followed. The monkeys parted to let them through.

Pig jumped into Pearly's arms, and the Woes threaded their arms around each other, staying at the entrance to the residence to watch the king confront his brother and take back control. It was a spectacular thing to witness.

Grandpa Woe's eyes filled with tears.

"Father, are you crying?" Ricky teased.

"Me, cry? No way, lad. High pollen count, I reckon." Grandpa Woe wiped his eyes and laughed, as Pearly's mother started giving her running commentary of the scene before them. And for Pearly, her mother's storytelling in full flight was a sure sign that everything was going to be okay.

"Will you look at that? Prince Keej just shoved Prince Tub over. No love lost there. Oh, look ... Princess Jong is having her say now. She is not happy with her uncle, that's for sure. I reckon she will make a wonderful queen one day ..."

Pearly didn't hear the rest. The mention of Princess Jong made Pig squirm, and Pearly remembered her jealousy and concern that Pig may not want to return to Orchard Island. Pearly let Pig down. "What's up?" she asked, though she was fearful of his answer.

I need to see Ma, Pig oinked. *We've been gone for days. I'm worried.*

Pearly felt heat race across her neck. All the time she had been worried about being stuck in the dungeon and jealous of the princess and not once did she think about how Pig might be worrying about his ma. She had done it again. Poor Pig. He deserved a better friend.

Pearly interrupted her mother's commentary to say, "We're going to check on Pig's ma, okay?"

"Hold on," said her father. "Is that wise? I mean, it could get–"

"Ricky!" warned her mother at the same time as Grandpa Woe said, "Son!"

"Sorry," said her father. "Old habits die hard. Say hello to her for me."

You don't have to come, Pig oinked.

"Of course, I do. She's your family, so that makes her my family too."

Pig gave her a piggy grin and the two skirted round

the edge of the compound, said a quick hello and thank you to Samam, before heading through the village towards Pig's ma's exile pen.

Already, things were changing in the village. Curious heads and even some smiling faces were poking out of the hut windows – all looking up to the compound and calling out to each other, trying to work out what was going on. Then like seeds in a spring breeze the news started to spread.

King Alung Chu is back!

The prince and princess too.

The jungle has spat them out!

They have returned to us.

Best of all was the joy in the news, the unmistakeable sound of happiness with a large dollop of hopefulness.

As they left the village and trotted along the track, Pearly hoped for Pig too – that he would receive welcome news as well.

And she wasn't disappointed.

Pig's ma was actually standing. Pig vaulted into the pen, and mother and son oinked their happiness rowdily. Pearly stayed back and watched. It was a tender moment. A bittersweet moment, as Pearly sensed that this is where Pig wanted to be, where he truly belonged.

And she knew.

Pig would not be returning with them to Orchard Island and Woe Mansion.

CHAPTER 33

By the time Pearly and Pig and Pig's ma had broken down the exile pen and tramped back to the village, the compound fence was in complete tatters. The compound was crowded with monkeys and elephants and pigs and chooks and excited villagers, shouting and cheering as Foom and Tub and Vam, and a long line of others were being marched out. King Alung Chu, it seemed, wasn't one to mull things over or to waste time.

A hush fell over the crowd as Pig's ma entered the compound. Hands were pressed together and heads were bowed as she passed.

"The Living Divine Sow has returned," shouted King Alung Chu, and he bowed too. Pig's ma sauntered up to the residence and sat down beside the doorway, as Pearly thought she had probably done many times before.

King Alung Chu approached Pearly. "Ah, Pearly. Can you help? Can you ask the monkeys to escort my brother and his family and guards? I want them off Anachak before nightfall."

Pearly looked at the long line marching out: all had baskets over their shoulders, and each were carrying a gold pig statue or pot or a carving of some sort.

"They're taking your valuables," Pearly said.

"I am not a cruel man. Foom is greedy and short-sighted, but he is still my brother and his children my family too. I do not want them to starve. And I do not want them to return. I gave them some time to collect their things and something to help them pay for their new life."

Just then Foom Chu turned, his round face smug. Pearly did not like the way he looked at his brother. He was definitely not one to be trusted. "But what if he does come back? What if he wants more? What if he brings outsiders in? What if–"

"They are not worries for today. They are only worries when or if they happen. Besides I have a plan. Tomorrow I will start work to make sure that the Sacred Statue of the Divine Sow is never disturbed again. We will protect her. Close up all the entrances and let the jungle do her work again. But now, I need your monkeys, and then it will be time to celebrate. My people need to sing and dance and eat until dawn."

Pearly sucked in a deep breath and craned her neck to seek out Wah-Wah. He had to be here somewhere –

she hoped he was, because he was her only chance to get the macaques' attention. And there he was sitting in the king's residence beside a huge basket of bananas. Of course.

Thank you, Wah-Wah, she chittered, as she caught the banana he chucked at her. *You know your monkey business. The king is grateful.*

Eat up, banana head, Wah-Wah chittered back.

The king wants the troop to escort Foom to the river.

Wah-Wah shoved the bananas into his mouth before chittering, *Tell king we like mangoes too. And lots of bananas. Always bananas.* And with that he sprang up to the rafters and swung into the compound, screeching and barking to the troop. The dominant male bounded up onto the roof of one of the huts, and jumped up and down, screeching, *To river. Take humans!*

Instantly, the macaques swarmed around the banished family, closing in tightly and noisily around them, giving them no chance of escape. The elephants joined the procession, and soon the tail end of the raucous line disappeared into the jungle, and the villagers erupted. They screamed and yelled, clapped and sang and cheered. Foom and Tub and the rest of the family were gone from Anachak forever, and with it went all the fear and sadness. There was only delight.

The true king had returned and the Sacred Statue of the Divine Sow was safe, and all was good again.

There was a tap on her shoulder and a boy about her age stood behind her holding a ball made up of tightly twisted vines. "Come play," he said in Anachakan. The boy dropped the ball and kicked it to Pearly.

Play? Pearly had never played with kids her own age before. On Orchard Island the Woes kept to themselves and stayed on the Woe Mansion estate. She had only ever played with Pig.

"Kick!" the boy encouraged.

Pearly gave the ball a kick, but only found air.

The boy smiled. "Kick ball!" he said.

Pearly kicked and struck the ball high into the air.

A mob of kids converged on it, pushing each other out of the way, until one kicked it out of the rabble, and they all gave chase. Pearly watched the ball as it bounced around the crowded compound. It flew right over Pig who was trotting around with his cousins. Trotting around happily, like he belonged. Pearly's heart dropped.

"Kick!" the boy yelled again. The ball had somehow made it back to her. Pearly thumped the ball and chased after it with the other kids.

Pearly sat near where Pig and his ma lay curled up sleeping. She was exhausted. Playing took a lot of energy. So did feasting on sticky rice and mangoes and noodle soup and whole fish cooked in coals.

It must have been close to midnight. Most of the animals had left, but the villagers showed no signs of tiring. A bonfire cast dancing shadows over those who were still frolicking and singing around it. A pale yellow moon and a twinkling sky smiled down on them.

Pearly leant back on her arms and took it all in. She watched as Grandpa Woe and King Alung Chu sat together in the king's residence chatting like the old pals they were. The relief on Grandpa Woe's face made Pearly smile. Her mother was sitting cross-legged nearby with a family, telling them in her broken Anachakan the story of their rescue by the monkeys. Her mum was back, and Pearly was glad. The prince and princess sat near the fire, both beating their hands rhythmically on drums perched on their laps. Her father was busily scribbling in his notebook. He had found Mu Savan – not in the way he expected, but Pearly knew that he would be trying to record every detail of it. He had fulfilled one of his lifelong dreams. He looked up from his notes and caught Pearly's eye. He closed his notebook, put his pencil into his shirt pocket and came to sit beside her.

"I'm so proud of you, Pearly," he said, and Pearly's eyes nearly shot out of their sockets with surprise. "But I'm not proud of myself. I kind of ... well, I panicked when things turned sour. Which surprised me, because I don't usually panic in sticky situations, but it seems I fall apart when the sticky situation involves you." He snuggled in close. "I'm sorry. I just worry about you and I let my worries get in the way."

"That's okay," Pearly said and meant it. "I'm an expert worrier, remember?"

Her father laughed, his face folding into happy creases around his mouth. "You know, you seemed not to worry so much during this adventure."

"Ha! Only about a million times!"

"Well, fancy that. You were busily worrying away, and you still had time to save the day."

"Me?"

"Pearly, you might be an expert worrier, but when you needed to act, you did. Your training kicked in and you were awesome."

Pearly drew her eyebrows together. "Why didn't you say so before now? You said I was being dangerous and a burden and a mistake ..."

"That was my bad. I wasn't being my best self – you were. I was the one who let my worries interfere with my judgement. You were so very brave, determined and ..." Her father rubbed her arm and drew her in closer.

"I certainly didn't help the situation, and I need to do better next time, but truly Pearly, you need to have more trust in your abilities. You don't need me to tell you that. You need to know it for yourself, deep inside."

Pearly snuggled into her father's shoulder and turned his words over in her mind. Did her worrying about what her family thought hold her back? She chewed her bottom lip. "But I worry all the time – and I can't seem to stop," she said.

"We were all worried on this adventure," her father said. "Who wouldn't be? But let's not forget that you're not just expert at worries – you are expert with languages. You have such a special gift. We'd still be in that dank smelly dungeon without your gift."

"It did stink, didn't it?"

"It sure did. In fact, I think that stink has walked up my nostrils and decided to stay."

Pearly laughed herself silly at that and hugged her father tight. Her gift for languages had actually saved them. She had never thought about it like that before. Maybe she could be an Adventurologist one day.

CHAPTER 34

They had spent five days hanging out with the people of Ban Noa. Five glorious days of playing kick the ball, eating sticky rice, having speed banana eating contests with Wah-Wah and helping to cart stone to the entrance to Mu Savan, so the city could be closed off and the Sacred Statue of the Divine Sow safe for eternity. Five days of watching Pig with his ma – the current living Divine Sow – and seeing him enjoy the company of his cousins.

Now it was time to go.

They had said their goodbyes up at the village and only Pig and the king had come to send them off at the edge of the mighty Mekong. Pig hadn't said anything about staying behind, but Pearly knew in her heart that he wasn't coming with them, and she was struggling to keep her emotion from overwhelming her. *Smoky bacon*! How was she ever going to cope without Pig?

But as her mother pushed their longboat into the muddy river, Pig was the first to clamber on board. Grandpa Woe was hugging King Alung Chu goodbye, her father was holding the boat steady and Pig was oinking at her to hurry up.

Pearly was confused.

"Aren't you staying?" Pearly asked Pig.

Staying? Why would I do that?

"But ..."

But what? Don't you want me?

"Of course I want you, but don't you want to be with your ma, your cousins, your family?"

You are my family, Pearly. You know that! Besides, I'd miss Angel's pizzas and corn fritters too much. And honestly there's only so much cavorting around with a bunch of pigs one can take.

Pearly wiped the tears from her face, shrugged and climbed on board.

Pig nudged her with his snout. *You really are a banana head, aren't you?*

She had to agree.

Pearly Woe had worried herself sick and heartsore about something that wasn't a worry at all. Fancy that. Wonders would never cease.

She sat with one hand across Pig at the back of the boat while her mother manoeuvred the boat from the shore and directed it up the river, once again in full commentary mode. Pearly gazed up at the lush jungle and the jagged limestone peaks poking through mashed potato clumps of cloud. She remembered how she had imagined that same jungle filled with rampaging T-rexes and swooping pterodactyls, and how she worried about venomous snakes and hungry tigers, killer ticks and strangler vines. Well, she had faced worse dangers than she could have ever imagined – marauding macaques on attack mode, a rogue king, a cliff fall, a stinky dungeon and an earthquake and more, but she had survived. She had not only survived, she had thrived. She had even saved a baby elephant calf and made new friends. And played with kids her age. She had faced the jungle and all that it threw at her and now she was going home. In one piece. And with Pig and her family of Adventurologists.

It hadn't been a walk in the park or smooth sailing. Far from it. And she hadn't always got it right. But that was okay.

Like her father, she'd do better on their next adventure. And there would be a next adventure.

She straightened her shoulders and breathed in the steamy jungle air, just as something hit her on the back of the head.

She clutched her head and swivelled round, expecting to see the pointy beak of a vulture coming in for its second shot, or a crocodile's tail thrashing about.

Instead, she found a banana on the deck of the boat.

Bah! Banana head! screeched a monkey voice from a palm tree on the shore.

Pearly laughed out loud.

Yep, she had to agree. She was definitely a banana head – and probably always would be.

THE
RULES AND GUIDELINES
FOR YOUNG ADVENTUROLOGISTS
(THE RAG)

BY GORDON WOE

THE ADVENTUROLOGISTS' GUILD

We are a top-secret group of stealth adventurers
founded by Gordon Woe in 1981. We love the thrill of
discovery and the challenge of going where no one has
gone before. We share a sense of awe and wonder at
our blue planet, and are driven to test our limits and to
search out unique experiences, but to do so quietly. We
take a solemn vow not to draw attention to ourselves,
gain profit, record, film or effect change during our
adventures. We are not showy TV adventurers. Respect
and care for the planet and its people are paramount.
Our reward is in meeting the challenge of the adventure
itself, of feeling wholly alive, and in satisfying our
human curiosity and craving for adrenaline.

The Guild was founded to provide a safe haven for like-minded adventurers, tired of flashy and fake modern-day adventurers and their destructive, self-serving, money-making ways. The Guild offers support and advice to its members, helps to raise funds when needed and trains young would-be Adventurologists.

THE CHARTER:
NO ADVENTURE TOO SMALL.
NO CHALLENGE TOO GREAT.
ADVENTURE BY STEALTH.
LEAVING NO TRACE.

RULES:

RULE 1: Stay alive.

RULE 2: Do not take or destroy.

RULE 3: Tread lightly.

RULE 4: Do not disturb the balance.

RULE 5: Never answer the Adventure Phone – unless an authorised member of the Adventurologists' Guild.

RULE 6: Respect the people you meet and the places you explore.

RULE 7: Never boast, brag, record or publicise your discoveries and adventures. Adventures are to be shared with the Guild only, and on a need-to-know basis.

ADVENTUROLOGING - THE BASICS

1. Be prepared. Planning is everything.
   Plan. Plan. Plan.
2. Be prepared, but also be prepared to be
   spontaneous, when plans don't go to plan.
3. Know your limits – and plan for this.
4. Push your limits – that's what adventurologing
   is all about.
5. Calculate your risks.
6. Good health and fitness is essential –
   both mind and body. Work hard at it.
7. Follow your passions, as they will guide you to
   the right places.
8. Take the time to savour the wonders you
   uncover – that's also what adventurologing
   is all about.

SURVIVING STICKY SITUATIONS

1. Take initiative.
2. Think outside the square.
3. Keep your eyes and ears open and your wits
   about you.
4. Make the impossible possible.
5. Think on your feet.
6. Act quickly and decisively.
7. Don't panic.
8. Logic is your friend.
9. Expect the unexpected.
10. Knowledge is power.

Pearly is a HYPERPOLYGLOT. That means she can speak many languages – twenty-seven in fact. What is particularly unusual about Pearly's gift for languages is that she can also speak some animal languages.

WOULD YOU LIKE TO SPEAK PIG?

Pearly's favourite animal language is, of course, Pig, because Pig is her best friend and she loves talking to him!

Pigs communicate with grunts and squeaks and squeals and oinks. They often sound raspy and gravelly and can be very noisy. Try these piggy words and phrases – some you would have already encountered in the story.

AROO, AROO, AROO = no direct translation, but indicates high levels of stress

GRICK = come on.

GRUNTITY-HUFF = clumsy

KRAR-KRAH *(two short snorts/grunts)* = goodbye

OINK OINK = hello

OINK-GOO-OINK = smoky bacon

OINKITY = no

OINKY OINKY NO-NO = trouble, I smell trouble

OINKY-SQUIO = horrible

RAH *(which sounds a bit like a short sharp snore or snort – tip: take short backwards-breath snort)* = yes

WOULD YOU LIKE TO SPEAK ELEPHANT?

Pearly's second favourite animal language is Elephant, because elephants have a lot to say and are fantastic communicators. She was so excited to be able to speak Elephant in this adventure in Anachak.

Elephants make a large range of noises from loud and sometimes long trumpeting and roaring to soft rumbly and gentle soothing noises. Try these elephant phrases.

BARR-WARRRRAHHH = goodbye and good luck

BRAH-ARAH = hold tight

BRRRR-BRRRR *(soft and gentle rumbling noise like a boat engine)* = no direct translation but is used to create calm.

RARARAH, RARARAH = Can I help?

ROWARRR! ROWARRR! ROWARRRRRR! = stay away

WAAAAARRRRRRRRRR = heeeellllppppp

WARRR *(spoken as a loud trumpeting noise, with trunk held high)* = help

WARRR-ORR-WARRR *(spoken with a loud screeching trumpet, flapping ears and stamping feet)* = halt or we'll trample you

WOULD YOU LIKE TO SPEAK MONKEY?

Wah-Wah the cheeky little macaque monkey helped Pearly improve her knowledge of Monkey.

Macaques make many sounds when they communicate. They chitter, chirp and bark, squeal, screech and scream. Sometimes they sound as if they are laughing. Body language, facial expressions and gestures are very important to them.

AHH-OOO-OOO-OOO = horrible

ARR-ARR-ARRRRR *(a high-pitched screech with lower teeth bared and glaring eyes)* = Fight!

ARR-ARR-GOO-GOO = banana head

BARI *(sharp and raspy bark made while jumping on the spot)* = go

ORR-ARR-ORR = clumsy

THE KINGDOM OF ANACHAK

The Kingdom of Anachak is an invented place, created from my imagination for Pearly and Pig's jungle adventure. If it actually existed it would be located somewhere in the rugged, inaccessible and jungle-covered hillsides along the banks of the Middle Mekong

River in Asia – probably within or close to the (real) Kingdom of Laos. (It is definitely not Laos, though.)

Anachak was inspired by my own adventures along the swirling muddy waters of Mekong River, where I travelled down the river in a longboat, just like the one the Woes travelled in, from Northern Thailand and into Laos. I visited remote villages and met many wonderfully inspiring people. I marvelled at the stunning landscapes and felt that I had entered a very special part of the planet, ancient, untouched and breathtakingly beautiful. That feeling stayed with me, and eventually found its way into my imagination and into this story.

As well as inventing the Kingdom of Anachak, I also invented the Anachakan language. Here are some phrases for you to try.

BAM HOON = got you

CHU-LA = pig (sacred animal to the Anachakans)

HELLO = sabba

LA-KAN = goodbye

NA YANYAN = horrible

YOOL = heave

PEARLY WOE IS A WORRIER.

She worries about anything and everything.
Mostly, she worries that her worries will mean
she will never become a member of the top-secret
group of stealth adventurers – The Adventurologists'
Guild – despite her very special talent of being
able to speak animal languages.

But with her parents missing, Pig pig-napped,
and Pearly a stowaway on an icebreaker heading
for Antarctica, Pearly's worries just got REAL.

ISBN 978 1 760653 59 0